S0-ADV-069

Double Trouble Squared

A STARBUCK FAMILY ADVENTURE

Double Trouble Squared

KATHRYN LASKY

Harcourt Brace Jovanovich, Publishers
San Diego New York London

Library of Congress Cataloging-in-Publication Data
Lasky, Kathryn.
Double trouble squared / by Kathryn Lasky.—1st ed.
p. cm.
Summary: In London with their family, telepathic twelve-year-old twins Liberty and July receive strange emanations from an early residence of Arthur Conan Doyle and discover a literary ghost.
ISBN 0-15-224126-4
ISBN 0-15-224127-2 (pbk.)
[1. Ghosts—Fiction. 2. Twins—Fiction. 3. Extrasensory perception—Fiction. 4. London (England)—Fiction.
5. Mystery and detective stories.] I. Title.
PZ7.L3274Do 1991
[Fic]—dc20 91-10655

Printed in the United States of America

First edition
A B C D E
A B C D E (pbk.)

For Linda Kime, my partner in literary crime

—K. L.

1

The House on Dakota Street

LIBERTY STARBUCK LEANED out the window of her bedroom. The third-floor room was round like a castle turret, and a big old tree grew in the front yard, shading half of the house. Liberty looked out through the tree's inky green leaves at the peaceful morning. She could hear the creak of the porch swing below, pushed by a whisper of wind.

And that whisper—did it echo another whisper somewhere deep in her mind? Liberty ran her hands through her hair.

She had been awake since sunrise, and it felt as if a voice in her dream had been speaking directly inside her brain—not a loud voice, just a whisper. But she could not remember the dream, and now even the whisper seemed to have vanished. Only a dim memory like an echo was left. She listened again, this time more attentively, to the wind pushing the swing.

All the other houses on Liberty's block were brick and had sharp corners. All the other big trees on the block were tulip trees or maples. But the Starbucks' house had two identical turrets, one cupola, and very few sharp corners. The tree that grew outside of Liberty Starbuck's curved window was not a tulip tree but an elm, one of the last in the entire county after the deadly elm epidemic decades before. And finally, the Starbucks' house was shingle, not brick. Despite the differences, Liberty thought, the Starbuck home probably seemed as peaceful as the next. Given your average Martian . . .

"Average Martian!" J. B. Starbuck burst through the connecting door to his twin sister's room. "What is an average Martian, Liberty?"

Liberty stared at her brother. His black hair slashed across his brow at the same steep angle as her own, except his slashed right, and hers slashed left. This morning his gray eyes were still foggy with sleep while hers were clear and alert. She had been up for half an hour already.

J. B. was short for July Burton, and a lot of people called him by his initials. A select few called him Jelly Bean. The twins had been born within five minutes of each other, during the first hour after midnight on the Fourth of July; that's why their parents named them July and Liberty.

"Martians should not be your concern this morning, Liberty," J. B. said.

"You mean Dad should?"

He nodded.

"I'm tired of Dad being our major concern. It's

getting boring, and"—she paused, her eyes worried—"it's scary."

July knew what she meant. It *was* scary. Things weren't normal anymore, and at first that was fun—having their dad home when they got home from school every afternoon, going grocery shopping with him, having him there to help with homework. But then it started to get a little frustrating.

Their father had been out of work just a week when he first sat down at the dining-room table where they always did their homework and announced he had some homework of his own—world work, he had called it. That was when he had started clipping things from the newspaper about environmental problems. There had been a lot that week about the ozone layer, and within two days their father knew all about it—so much that both twins decided to do a report on it for their Current Events class. They had a fight about that, however, when they realized they both couldn't do the same thing. So their father obligingly found them a second environmental problem—acid rain—and he began clipping articles like crazy for that one.

Liberty instead decided to do her report on the latest findings on twins that had been separated at birth, pairs that had grown up apart yet wound up drinking the same brand of beer, liking the same kinds of books, and wearing the same kinds of clothes. Sometimes when they married they even gave their children the same names without ever knowing it! Liberty had always been very interested in the science of twins—the biology of twins, the psychology of twins, even the mythology of twins. Twinology, as she called it, was one of her favorite areas of research.

It was good to have their dad helping them out with their reports and doing all this research, but it was unsettling, too. It was hard to explain to friends when they came in and saw him at home. There he would be, sitting at the table with them—the twins doing their homework, their father clipping at newspapers, doing his world work. How could they explain a father who did world work? Everybody else on the street had a father who left the house to go to work. And most of them had a mother who left for work, too.

"He doesn't exactly seem worried enough, does he?" J. B. said.

"He doesn't seem worried at all," Liberty replied.

"Mom seems worried."

"Yeah, sort of."

"But he seems so happy about being out of work."

"Well, he's going to drive us nuts with all his new ideas. If I hear him use the word 'explore' one more time, I'm going to barf." Liberty paused and bit her lip lightly. "What about that London job?" she asked.

"It's, like, too good to hope for."

"What do you mean hope? It's an offer."

"But it's too complicated with Mom not being able to go except once a month. No way can she run the factory from three thousand miles away."

Their mother, Madeline Starbuck, was the largest

manufacturer of ballet tutus in the United States. But she made more than tutus. She specialized in recital wear. This meant everything from leotards and tutus to splashy sequin numbers with all the accessories. There were more than five thousand ballet schools in North America, and Madeline Starbuck had a definite corner on the market. A large percentage of those five thousand schools bought exclusively from the Starbuck "Show Time" catalog for their annual recitals. In fact, their mother essentially choreographed these recitals each year through her cleverly designed costumes. If her suppliers were long on dotted spandex and tulle, Madeline thought "Gumdrops!" and that June across the country, thousands of four-year-olds waddled out on stages from Trenton to Tacoma to do the Gumdrop Dance in their dotted costumes.

J. B. was right. It was a business that could not simply be left three thousand miles behind so Madeline Starbuck could follow her husband to London, where he had been offered the post of under secretary to the ambassador to the Court of St. James. And even if she were able to go, who would take care of the four Starbuck children?

Liberty and J. B. had two younger sisters, Charly and Molly, who were also twins—identical five-year-old girls. In the twins business, Charly and Molly were what was known as mirror-image identicals. This meant that while one twin was left-handed, the other was right-handed; that while they both had the same spiky red hair, which stuck out all over their heads most of the time, Charly's cowlicks swirled clockwise, while Molly's swirled counterclockwise. Molly had a tiny strawberry mark on her right earlobe, and Charly had one on her left. It was as if they were reflections of one another—mirror images.

Mirror-image twins happen only once for every three hundred fifty sets of identical twins born. Although they weren't mirror-image twins, Liberty and July were about as identical as a twin brother and sister could get: the same hair, except Liberty wore hers in a ponytail, and July's fell shaggy around his ears; the same bands of freckles across their noses; and the same luminous gray eyes fringed with dark lashes. They even had the same dimple that flashed when they spoke.

Brother-and-sister twins were rarely as physically identical as July and Liberty. And for one family to have two sets of twins, one pair mirror-image and one pair almost identical, was against all odds.

So if one were to add in the elm tree and the shingled house, the Starbucks were a statistically rare family. One might say a singular family if it were not for two pairs of twins. What made it uncomfortably singular this morning was that this was the only house on the block where the father was out of work.

"Well," said Liberty, "I hope London isn't too much to wish for."

"Me, too!"

J. B. went back to his own room in the second turret. It was connected to Liberty's by a small hallway. On the way, he looked wistfully at the sculpted bronze bust of Sherlock Holmes that occupied a table opposite his door. As sunlight streamed down through the curved window, the head was crosshatched with glints and gleams, and the dark eyes took on a strange intensity that . . . well . . .

J. B.'s breath locked in his throat. He stepped closer to the head and looked again. No, the eyes had not flickered, but the features suddenly appeared more expressive, and the entire face seemed to possess something no ordinary artist could have sculpted. And a *very* ordinary artist had made this sculpture. J. B.'s mother had bought the bust at a roadside souvenir shop for ten dollars. It wasn't even real bronze, and there had been at least twenty others identical to this one.

J. B. backed away. Shadows seemed to gather around the eyes again. The head looked quite normal once more. Undoubtedly his imagination had been working overtime. Still he was left with a slightly uncomfortable feeling.

Those glints and gleams had reminded him of something else. What was it? He thought for a moment. If Liberty had still been upstairs, it might have dawned on him quicker . . . but yes, of course! That was it! It had to do with the telepathy he and his sister shared.

The twins—all four—had always been able to communicate telepathically. The current was strongest on the two-way circuit within each set. But it was by no means a closed circuit, and sometimes all four of them communicated with one another, even though there was usually a bit of static.

But now something had changed. It was not as if the quality of the telepathy was worse in any way; if anything, it seemed to be better. In fact, it was so much better that Liberty and July seemed to be picking up other signals, not really complete messages or even fragments of messages, but rather dim echoes.

But from where? The echoes, if indeed that's what they were, were not echoes of familiar sounds, but shadows of something strange and unknown.

J. B. knew Liberty had sensed these echoes, too. He could just tell, by the breaks in her own telepathic thought. These breaks were completely in sync with his own when they happened. It was as if something else was trying to push in. Another consciousness? No, no, more like an echo, and they were both straining to hear it together.

Yet they never spoke of it, either telepathically or out loud. He wasn't sure why, but there was something vaguely disturbing, invasive about it.

J. B. tried not to worry about it. With Dad acting so weird lately, he had more immediate things to think about. Besides, so little was known about telepathy, maybe this was perfectly normal. Things change, J. B. told himself. After all, he and Liberty were growing up. This change in their telepathic communication could be a sign of puberty, right? If the body could change, why couldn't this? Seemed perfectly reasonable.

He went over to the mirror above his dresser and leaned close. He searched his upper lip. Darn! Last week he could have sworn he saw a shadow there. Was it just dirt? Not a mustache? He grabbed the magnifying glass he kept on the windowsill and held it between his upper lip and the mirror. He studied the skin above his lip minutely. He could almost feel the sculpted head of Holmes looking at him over his shoulder. Its blank eyes were cloaked in shadows—were they laughing at him?

Not a hair! Oh well, what did he care. He was much too young to be sprouting facial hair. There were only a few girls he liked anyway. And you didn't need to have a mustache to like a girl. Oh man! This was a stupid conversation he was having with himself. He was glad Liberty was downstairs, out of range.

J. B.'s own deerstalker cap had fallen off the top of the sculpted head where he kept it. Now he tossed it back.

Both July and Liberty loved Sherlock Holmes. And to think they were so close to moving to London, the setting for so many of the great detective's adventures—the city where the author of the Sherlock Holmes tales, Sir Arthur Conan Doyle, had lived!

J. B. grabbed a baseball cap from his bedpost and headed out of his room and down to breakfast. On the second floor, he passed Charly and Molly's room. They were dawdling.

Charly and Molly were Olympic dawdlers. They could find more things to do in the course of getting dressed in the morning than most people found to do in a whole day. Charly was lying on the floor twirling her sock over her face. Molly was rolling a marble through one of the tunnels of the Toilet Roll Kingdom, a city they had built for their toilet roll people. He sighed as he looked in, then went down the stairs. What world problem would Dad be trying to solve this morning? Yesterday it had been bacon and ozone layer over lightly; today Cheerios with bananas and . . .

"White Band Disease!" The words rolled ominously over the top edge of the *Washington Post*. From behind the newspaper a hand reached for a mug of coffee. The paper lowered a bit, and the top of a bald head shone. Then two intelligent but sober eyes appeared from behind half-spectacles. "Hear that, J. B.?"

"What, Dad?"

"White Band Disease." Putnam Starbuck paused dramatically. "And it's not a rock group. It's something everyone should know about."

"What is it?"

Did you have to ask? He felt Liberty teleflash the question.

"A plague . . . and it's attacking the elkhorn coral of the Caribbean. It has actually struck from Colombia to Venezuela and as far north as Florida," Put replied. "Don't they do anything to promote environmental awareness and education in your school?" He looked sharply at J. B.

"Well, you know, they teach a little bit, about the normal stuff, but not about White Band Disease."

"Well, what about fluorocarbons?" Put leaned forward.

"What about them?" Liberty asked.

"Is there any sort of active campaign to educate students and their families about the dangers of aerosol cans to the ozone layer?"

"Uh . . . not that I know of," Liberty said.

"Hmmm." Put leaned back in his chair and picked up his coffee cup. His eyes seemed distant, as if he was contemplating something far away. Liberty and July both got a funny sinking feeling.

"Oh dear!" Madeline Starbuck was wearing running shoes and running shorts, and she was jogging through the kitchen with a fried egg in a small skillet and a bagel. She didn't jog for pleasure or for exercise. She only ran in her kitchen, and that was because in the morning she was always in a rush. When the children left for school, she would slip into the laundry room and get dressed for work. She always wore her running shoes to work, too, and kept a dress-up pair of shoes at her office for important meetings when she had to look tall, tough, and fashionable. Otherwise she looked simply short and sensible.

"Now, as I understand it," Madeline said, delivering the fried egg and bagel to her husband, "you, my dear, are going to be responsible for dinner tonight."

"Right. What time did you invite Honey for?"

"Honey!" Liberty and J. B. chorused.

"Mom, is Aunt Honey coming for dinner?" Liberty wailed.

"Yes, dear. Don't whine—she tries to be nice."

"Sometimes," J. B. muttered.

"Well, we have to break the news to her about Dad," Madeline said.

"She doesn't know about Dad yet? Where's she been for the last three weeks?"

"Out of the country, on vacation," their mother replied.

"Madeline, what do you mean—break the news?" Putnam Starbuck snapped his paper shut and folded it in two quick movements. "I was not fired. My resignation was not asked for. There is nothing shameful about quitting a job because of principles. Must I remind you?"—the children knew exactly what was coming—"*Sui Veritas Primo!*" Put said the words solemnly. It was the Starbuck family motto. It translated roughly as Truth to Self First. It had not been handed down through generations on a coat of arms. It had been invented, Latin and all, by Putnam Starbuck.

"I don't mean to sound high-minded about this," Put continued, "but more people in this town should think about their principles. If they did, we wouldn't need so many grand jury investigations and special congressional committees on ethics. Not to mention those white-collar prisons where government employees caught doing dirty tricks go to play golf for their prison terms."

"Of course, dear." Madeline ran her fingers across his head. If there had been hair there, it probably would have looked like a more soothing gesture, but there wasn't. Put was bald, shiny bald, on top. And he did not seem soothed by his wife's stroking.

Liberty and July looked nervously at each other. Would this lead to an argument?

"I really resent this attitude on the part of my family. I am looking at this as a time of great exploration and growth and new discovery."

Liberty looked over her cereal bowl, straight at her father. Vasco da Gama he's not, she thought.

"But of course, dear, about dinner tonight," Put continued. "I shall make the dinner. It will all be ready." He smiled stiffly, almost mechanically. J. B. caught a glimpse of it out of the corner of his eye and looked deeper into his Cheerios.

"Remember, no meat."

Not a simple chop? Liberty's eyes flew open. Had she said that?

Chop, chop of what? July teleflashed.

My thoughts precisely, she replied.

You said it. Don't you know?

I know I said it. I mean, I guess I did.

Are you trying to say you don't know what you're talking about?

No, no, of course not. I said it. I just don't know why.

"Chop" was simply not a word in Liberty's vocabulary, at least not in the way she had just said it. But had she actually said it? She thought again of that whisper of the wind pushing the front-porch swing and those dim echoes that had pressed her from sleep so early.

"How could I forget?" Put said. "Your sister has been a vegetarian forever."

Chop. July continued to turn the word over in his mind. It had a ring to it, an echo. *Yes, of course!*

Of course what? Liberty asked.

Think about the way English people talk—like Sherlock, for example. They never say "a slice of roast beef" or "a hamburger patty."

They didn't have hamburger patties then, Liberty retorted. Yet she felt a shiver crawl up her spine.

That's not the point. They always talk about chops. There's that fancy restaurant that Mom and Dad go to—the London Chop House.

Liberty didn't want to hear anything about it. She turned her attention back to what her mother was saying.

"Being a vegetarian is a matter of principle on my sister's part," Madeline said pointedly and smiled at Put. Another stiff little smile.

Liberty and J. B. looked at each other again. Their parents weren't yelling exactly, but this was just as bad—poking each other with little toothpick swords. Both twins toyed with their soggy Cheerios. Liberty felt a twinge in her stomach.

She felt caught in a cross fire between the razor-sharp voices of her parents' bickering and those dim echoes. Where were they coming from?

"No meat," Put reiterated.

"No meat!" Charly screamed as she ran into the kitchen.

Molly followed, yawning, and asked, "Aunt Honey's coming for dinner?"

"You guessed it," J. B. said.

"Mercy, mercy, mercy!" Molly said. Their mother had been reading them *Little House on the Prairie*, and that was one of Ma's favorite expressions.

"Why doesn't Aunt Honey like meat?" Charly asked.

"Because she thinks it makes you aggressive and violent and generally disgusting," Liberty said.

She is disgusting, all four twins thought together.

How did Charly and Molly know not to say it aloud? J. B. wondered.

Who knows? Who cares? They didn't—that's what counts, Liberty replied in a silent flash.

I think I'm getting indigestion—White Band Disease, Aunt Honey, Cheerios! It's all too much on an empty stomach.

And don't forget the snot—when will Charly and Molly learn to wipe their noses?

Shut up! both the little twins flashed. Charly began to raise her right arm as Molly raised her left.

"Not on your sleeves, girls!" Madeline cried and jogged over with Kleenex and two bowls of Cheerios.

2

The War on Fluorocarbons and Other Disasters

FOR THE LIFE OF HIM, J. B. could not remember the exact shapes of the Great Lakes. This was the first question on the geography test. He just had too much other stuff on his mind.

He hated it when his parents bickered, and that scowl his mother had given his father made him feel like he had eaten something sour. And then there was this London thing. Why did it have to be so complicated?

Stop with London, he ordered himself. It's the Great Lakes you've got to think about right now. But if he couldn't get the shapes right, he'd have a heck of a time getting all those states around them. He was in trouble, and he knew it. He couldn't afford to have a low grade on this test.

Suddenly there was a glint, and a twinkling outline flickered in his mind's eye. Liberty was teleflashing him an image, a shape.

You've got Lake Huron all wrong! It's got a thumb

that sticks out on the southwest side—Saginaw Bay—and then there's this blob on the northeast side. That's Georgian Bay.

Thanks a million, Liberty!

Okay. Now that you've got that straight, kindly tell me—what is the capital of Minnesota?

Liberty, I can't believe it. The Twin Cities, idiot!

The message flashed diagonally across the room from J. B. in the back to Liberty in the front. No interference from Chelsea Cohen's newly permed hair, which stuck out a few light years from her head.

Which one, stupid? That's my problem. St. Paul or Minneapolis?

Mental telepathy was particularly useful in school during tests. The twins did not consider it cheating. It was just part of the way their minds worked. Liberty was better at seeing whole pictures, large configurations, and patterns. J. B. was better at understanding the small parts within a pattern or a picture. Together the twins made a good team. But as skillful as he was with small parts, J. B. still worried about certain small things like the scowl on his mom's face, and the pointed way his father had said "But of course, dear" when he agreed to make dinner for Aunt Honey.

You've got to stop this worrying, J. B. It's interfering with your schoolwork. Dad's problems aren't ours.

Can you believe this!

It was fifth period. And on Wednesdays fifth period was always school assembly. The geography test had been over for more than an hour. July and Liberty never could have anticipated what would follow after Mr. Zoltrono, the principal, made his announcement over the PA system. At assembly that morning there would be a guest who would talk to the students about a very special and exciting project.

I don't believe ☆#3!☆ this! July, do you see what I see? July and Liberty were sitting rows apart in the auditorium. The quality of their telepathy was fairly jagged, with lots of static, because of their high anxiety level and the acute embarrassment they were suffering. For Putnam Starbuck was walking on stage with Mr. Zoltrono.

Why hadn't their father warned them? Or had he, in his own way? The ceaseless talk about the ozone layer, the rising temperatures of the world, the coral disease in the Caribbean, his questions about their schooling in environmental issues—should all of this evidence have tipped them off?

"Boys and girls," Mr. Zoltrono began, "our featured speaker could not make it today. So we are lucky that one of our local residents was able to make last-minute plans to come talk to us about a very important subject. As you might know, one of the great environmental hazards afflicting our planet today is our damaged ozone layer."

Oh . . . gosh . . . this . . . xy #3### embarras+ + + + Dad . . . never %%%%~~~~~ can't be ''''''''''!!!!!!! Holy moly !!!!!!*

"It is my great privilege," Mr. Zoltrono continued, "to introduce to you our speaker for today"—

Privilege Privil@@@@

"Hello, children," Putnam was saying. Liberty and July slumped in their seats. It was so embarrassing to have their father up there calling three hundred fifty kids, who all knew them, "children."

I mean, has this man been a kid in the last thousand years? July's message got through clearly this time.

"I am asking you," Putnam went on, "to join me in what I am calling the War on Fluorocarbons." He was holding aloft an aerosol can of deodorant.

Did he have to use a deodorant can? Why not at least hairspray or Lysol? Liberty had never experienced such agony.

"I am asking you in the next two weeks to collect all the cans you can find and join me in a march. Two weeks from this Saturday, on June second, we shall proceed down Pennsylvania Avenue, past the White House, then up to the Capitol. On the steps of the Capitol we shall deposit our collection of aerosol cans. And remember, children, our slogan: 'Some cans are returnable, but our planet is not!' "

Oh drat, he must have been up all night thinking up that one!

Jeez Louise! Is this child abuse or what?

How can he be doing this to us?

I don't know. I don't care. We have to get him to take the London job. No matter what.

It lasted longer than a shot at the doctor's office, and no one told July and Liberty they were brave afterward, even though they didn't cry. But they did consider exile. Little scenarios ran through their heads—moving in with their favorite babysitter, Zanny Duggan. Running away to London without their parents.

At recess both July and Liberty raced to the office phone.

"This is an emergency, Iris. If Mom's in a meeting, get her out!" Liberty nearly shouted at Iris Wetzel, their mother's secretary. "This is so humiliating," Liberty muttered. "This is worse than that time we had to go ice skating with Aunt Honey, and she was whirling around on the ice in that dumb outfit with her big fat butt hanging out!—Hello, Mom . . . it's us."

"Nobody's dead!" July yelled into the phone from behind Liberty.

"But if embarrassment could kill, you'd have two dead kids. Mom, do you know what Dad did today?"

Liberty quickly explained.

"No!" Madeline was aghast. "Oh dear! I knew Mr. Zoltrono called this morning, but I had no idea why. It didn't sound important. Oh *dear*. Well, okay. Now don't you worry. I'm going to set my mind to this. Daddy just needs to get involved in something, but I understand he doesn't have to involve you."

July grabbed the phone. "I mean, Mom, it's not that Liberty and I are for fluorocarbons and against the ozone layer, but I mean, does Dad have to bring his war or march or whatever he calls it right into our school?"

Liberty grabbed the receiver back. "I got news for you, Mom. We're going to die of terminal embarrassment. It's going to get us before the ozone layer. Dad's got to take that job in London no matter what!"

3

The Honey Pit

"I DO THINK, Put, that this London offer is a wonderful opportunity."

"But darling, we'd hardly get to see each other. It would be a commuter marriage."

"I know it would require sacrifice, but good marriages do require sacrifice. And I think it's best that the kids go with you—I'm just too busy at the factory this time of year to be able to take care of them here if you'll be gone. It'll be good for them, too, to see what life is like in another country. And I know there's a way we could figure out the child care. There has to be somebody."

Liberty and July exchanged a relieved glance. They were up on the landing.

"So the kids were really upset about me coming to school?"

"Well, yes, a bit."

A *bit*, J. B. cracked silently. *That's the understatement of the millenium.*

Cool it, she's just trying to play her cards right. The point is to get to London.

You're right.

At that moment both twins glanced toward J. B.'s bedroom. He had left the light on, and the shadow of Sherlock Holmes's sculpted head stretched out over the floor. The deerstalker's hat seemed three feet tall, and the pipe clenched between Sherlock's teeth looked at least a foot long.

It had started to rain outside. Big drops splashed against the windowpanes. But there was something beating in Liberty's head. She squeezed her eyes shut.

You're hearing it, aren't you? J. B. flashed. Liberty's eyes shut tighter. *Like echoes.*

Yes, yes, she finally acknowledged. *It's like the raindrops on the window . . . that's how the echoes beat inside. You, too? I can't believe it.*

Suddenly a door opened—the front door downstairs.

"Hello!" a voice trilled. "It's absolutely sopping out there." The rain in their heads stopped instantly.

"Honey!"

Ugh!

Aunt Honey glided across the living-room floor to embrace her twin sister.

No set of twins had ever been as different as Honey and Madeline. Honey had hair bright as brass and big gleaming eyes made bigger by thick globs of mascara. Madeline had black hair flecked with gray, and brown eyes unadorned by mascara. She was three inches shorter and seven minutes younger than Honey.

Although Honey had retired from the Ice Capades almost five years before, she still seemed to have her skates on. She always appeared to glide. And there was always that phony megawatt smile on her face. Whatever had been beating on the windowpanes of their brains had recoiled completely with the arrival of Aunt Honey.

"Children!" Madeline called upstairs. "Aunt Honey is here."

Brace yourself, Liberty flashed.

Or maybe put on your skates—one never knows how to play it with Aunt Honey, J. B. replied. Charly and Molly were already downstairs.

As Liberty hit the last step, Aunt Honey spun around. She smiled broadly. "Aren't we getting to be a big girl now! Soon we'll be developing."

This was beyond belief. This jerk-aunt-ice-bunny! Liberty began to have the most violent thoughts, and J. B. hid a smile.

But Madeline quickly deflected the conversation. No sense wasting time. "Honey, we have a little announcement to make." Her sister blanched visibly under all the makeup.

"Oh no, Madeline. You can't be pregnant again! Another set will kill you."

How do you like that, guys? July barked telepathically. *We're sets: interchangeable, indistinguishable, all parts included, very little assembly required.*

And we're killers! Molly almost wailed out loud, but managed by great dint to keep her distress within telepathic channels.

"No such thing." Madeline smiled brightly. "Put has left the CIA."

"Put has what!" Honey was stunned. "Tell me what I'm hearing isn't so!"

"But it is, and we're very pleased."

"He left the Central Intelligence Agency?" Aunt Honey sputtered. "That's the most ridiculous thing I've ever heard. Why? Why? Why in heaven's name did you leave?"

So there, fat face! Charly telepathically growled while giving the sweetest little dimpled smile to her aunt. This was not lost on Aunt Honey. She reached over and gave Charly's chubby freckled cheek a distracted pinch.

"Is that a face!" she cooed.

No, Aunt Honey. It's a foot! July sighed. Then Charly giggled out loud and telepathically at the same time, which made the air between the four children sizzle.

Would you all shut up! Liberty flashed a warning. *I'm trying to concentrate on Dad's response to this, and I can't with all your crackling. It's like being in the middle of an electrical storm.*

Their father took a deep breath. "I quit for a very simple reason, Honey. My principles."

"Your principles!" Aunt Honey shrieked. "What does that have to do with anything? What could the CIA ever have asked you to do that would have hurt your principles?"

"They asked him to do the unthinkable," Madeline said softly.

"Murder?" Honey's voice seemed almost bright with expectation.

"Oh, for heaven's sake!" Put scoffed.

"Well, what did they ask you to do that got you to give up a perfectly decent job?"

"They asked me to do what Madeline so aptly described as the unthinkable—to subvert my identity."

Liberty and J. B. could tell their father was getting steamed now, just the way he had been when he had come home from the office three weeks before.

"They wanted him to wear a wig and use a voice changer," Madeline said wearily.

"And you wouldn't do that?" Honey was aghast. "What's the big deal?"

"To hide what you are is a big deal in my book, Honey. *Sui Veritas Primo*, truth to self. That is our family motto. I have worked at the agency for ten years. I had thought we understood each other and my requirements for working there. They know I am extremely uncomfortable with the cloak-and-dagger aspects of the agency, but they originally asked me to do what I do best—be a mediator in the department and a liaison with Congress. And that is what I have done until now."

"Well, I don't understand what's so terrible about all this. Why did they want you to wear a wig and use a voice changer?"

"You know I can't divulge that information, Honey."

"I think we should move into the dining room," Madeline said. "Dinner's ready, isn't it, Put?"

"Yes."

Liberty and J. B. had just brought in the last plates and were sitting down. The main course was spaghetti covered with a buttery sauce and all sorts of bright vegetables. Charly's and Molly's plates looked a little different. They didn't like food that "touched." So they each had a mound of plain spaghetti in the middle and separate little piles of vegetables heaped around the edges of their plates like colorful satellites.

"Is that cerise tutu with the ostrich feathers I test-skated for you still your number-one seller?" Honey asked.

"Well, yes, with certain schools, and of course the ice shows still order it yearly."

"It was rather ingenious—that idea of knitting in the feathers—if I do say so myself."

"Well, Honey, I've always said if it holds up on ice, it will hold up anyplace."

"Ah, yes." She smiled.

She's always taking credit for Mom's business.

She's jealous of Mom. She can't stand it that Mom has made all that money on her own, and she's only made it from marrying rich guys, J. B. answered.

"Delish! Madeline!" exclaimed Aunt Honey as she took a bite.

Why can't she just say the whole word? Liberty wondered.

Don't pay any attention to her.

How can you ignore her?

"I didn't make it," Madeline was saying. "This is all Putnam's doing."

"When does Putnam have the time?"

Now that really galled Liberty. *Why does she think Mom has more time than Dad when Mom has to work all day and has to drive all the way to Chevy Chase, and Dad only had a ten-minute commute to his office?*

I told you. She's jealous of Mom. Elementary, my dear Liberty, as Sherlock would say.

At that moment they both thought of the shadow cast upstairs and barely heard the tinkle of Honey's laughter.

"I forgot. You're unemployed now. Plenty of time to cook." Honey picked up her water glass and sighed wearily. "Oh dear, Put. I hope this isn't a mistake on your part. That was a wonderful job. You'd been there forever. You were a senior man. I was so proud of you, of having a brother-in-law working in this, the most sacred branch of our government."

Sacred! Liberty silently exclaimed.

Separation of church and state. That was our first civics lesson. Where was Aunt Honey for fifth-grade civics? J. B. wondered.

Doing double-axle spins with the Three Stooges.

They both giggled at their silent telejoke.

Suddenly Liberty and July felt a silvery shimmer in their heads, a dim, dim echo—almost like a cascade of thin coins raining down in a tinkly patter. Or was it almost laughter?

You heard it, too? Liberty teleflashed.

Was somebody else laughing? I mean, it was funny, but not that funny.

What do you mean, not that funny? Liberty asked. She knew July was not being critical.

I'm not sure, he answered honestly. *I think I meant that it was not so funny that . . . that . . .* He groped for some kind of meaning.

That somebody outside the family would get it, let alone hear it. Liberty finished his thought.

But you heard it in your head, didn't you?

I . . . I . . . I'm not sure. It's like I'm not sure whether I heard it or felt it. I keep thinking of the rain outside beating inside my . . .

"They're doing it again," Aunt Honey snapped, glaring at Liberty and J. B.

"Doing what?" Putnam asked.

"That mental stuff of theirs," she growled.

Sounds like a meat eater to me! J. B. flashed.

They both stifled another giggle by loading forkfuls of spaghetti into their mouths.

"You mean telepathy?" Madeline asked mildly.

"Precisely. It's very unsociable, and I know they do it about me. The little set, too."

Madeline hated it when people referred to her children as sets, but she ignored it. "This spaghetti smells as good as it tastes. I just love that garlic." She bent over her plate, inhaled deeply, and tried not to think about how much her sister really did irritate her.

Honey was right. The "little set" was talking about her. They liked her thick orange lipstick. They didn't like much else about her.

I don't smell just the garlic. I smell . . .

Lipstick! Molly finished Charly's thought.

Look at those big smoochy marks Aunt Honey's lipstick leaves on the water glass. Both twins sniffed.

"Oh dear. Are you two coming down with colds?"

"No!" they both blurted out.

"Just smelling the garlic," Charly said quickly.

What a diplomat! Liberty chimed in telepathically. Neither Liberty nor J. B. could pick up the word-for-word translation of the telepathic exchange between Molly and Charly, but they knew it had something to do with orange lipstick and how it smelled.

Personally, I prefer the garlic, J. B. flashed. *The lipstick is totally yucky.* The little twins got it.

It is not! they both silently blurted. The channels were now more fully opened between the older twins and the younger ones, and each word was coming through clearly. It usually took only a matter of seconds for all four twins to be able to cross-communicate clearly. There was just a bit of a time lag. Like the signal delay in satellite communication, their words came through clearly, but just a split second late when all four of them were teleflashing together.

She puts it on so thick, Molly was saying, *that you can smell it even through the garlic—kind of sweet and creamy.*

A little bit soapy . . . and look. See? Some stuck to that piece of spaghetti that she's slurping up now.

Yuck! Liberty and July both flashed.

"Honey, I don't think we've told you about the wonderful job offer Put is seriously considering," Madeline said.

Wonderful job offer! Seriously considering. The air became static with teleflashed excitement. Those words "seriously" and "considering" were music to their ears. And if Mom was mentioning it to Honey, it must be serious.

She's not just saying this to please Aunt Honey, is she?

She can't be, J. B. replied.

Madeline and Put proceeded to explain the job offer to Honey.

"Yes—under secretary to the ambassador in London, Court of St. James. My focus would actually be environmental issues, which, of course, would be pleasing."

"It's really like being an under ambassador," Madeline added proudly.

The children, all four of them, were concentrating so hard they barely heard the words. They had to convince their father that he could do it, that the problems were minor. They wanted this to happen more than anything, all four of them, all five of them if you included Madeline—all six of them if you included the shadow upstairs.

Oh, let it happen! they all flashed in unison, for even Charly and Molly somehow sensed this was vitally important.

"Put! How marvelous! Why haven't you said yes immediately?"

Oh, say yes! Like a silent chant the children's telepathic signals seized the air. *Say yes, Daddy! Make it be!*

"Well, Honey, there are problems with moving an entire family to London. For one thing, Madeline obviously could not come, except occasionally. We've decided it would be best if the children were to come with me—a great experience for them. But this means they would be without their mother, and even if we could arrange for child care . . ."

"Look," Aunt Honey said, "I think this job offer in London sounds wonderful. And I don't think you should dismiss it just because of the child-care problem. But it's summer now, so that is a bit hard in terms of what to do with them."

She makes us sound like we're the classroom gerbils, or something that has to be taken care of over the school vacation, Liberty teleflashed.

We're not gerbils! Charly and Molly silently blurted.

"But," Aunt Honey continued, "I don't see why I couldn't come and help you out for just a few weeks, until you've found someone over there, you know. I mean England of all places—they invented nannies.

They have nanny schools. I can take care of the children for a few weeks and help you interview nannies."

The twins were horrified. Imagine who Aunt Honey would pick as a nanny if, indeed, they even survived her. But their parents were looking across the table at one another as if they thought this was a perfectly reasonable idea. The twins suddenly realized they were in real danger. The unthinkable was actually happening!

Seconds before, the air had been crackling with the electricity of their telepathic communications. But now it was still. And as the realization sunk in, a sickening feeling of powerlessness overwhelmed each child. They felt indeed as if they were falling into a bottomless pit—a Honey pit!

They were tumbling out of control, and it seemed there was absolutely nothing they could do to reverse the fall.

4

Zanny the Nanny

ZANNY DUGGAN had parked a block away and begun to stroll toward Dakota Street on this fine Saturday morning. The air was balmy, and the smell of things young and green filled the breeze. It was hard to rush, even though the messages on her answering machine from July and Liberty had sounded rather desperate: "It's not a fate worse than death but a pretty close second," July's voice had squeaked with anxiety. "Just imagine Aunt Honey babysitting us for three weeks!"

Then Liberty's voice had come on in a second message.

"Wouldn't you like never to have to deal with that miserable principal of Springdale School again? Wouldn't you like never to have to teach another child of the Kendall family—admit it, Zanny, you said you had never met a child you didn't like, and then you met Sammy Kendall, and then the next year Lucy Kendall, and then Davy Kendall, and you know we overheard you tell your mom that they were the most disgusting children. Every teacher in your entire school dreads getting them, and there's a very good chance you could get Randy Kendall next year—"

Liberty had exceeded the message time on the tape at this point, so she had to call back. "Would you not instead—as opposed to those disgusting children—prefer the lovely, engaging, and absolutely terrific Starbuck children—known for their wit, charm, elegant manners, and all this in an exotic setting—London?"

July's and Liberty's words streamed through Zanny's mind along with thoughts of spring and the end of school. The twins could not have known that she was thinking of telling her principal she wouldn't be back in the fall. Or could they? Somehow they often seemed to know such things. She rounded the corner onto Dakota Street and heard the metallic clank of wagon wheels coming down a short dead-end street that dipped from a high hill. Suddenly a red blur hurtled toward her. In the wake of the wagon, a dog barked furiously.

"Charly! Molly!"

Zanny Duggan lowered herself slightly, hunched over, spread her arms, and assumed the posture of a hockey player guarding the goal. The red wagon and the little twins—wild-eyed and hair stiff with mousse—crashed right into her. They all crumpled into a heap. Yapping around the tangle of legs and upturned wagon wheels was a dog that appeared to be mad. Yet the dog, a Welsh terrier, was not foaming at the mouth. Instead it was foaming on top of its wiry and strangely cropped head.

"What in the world!" Zanny sputtered and got up, shaking out her skirt. "Would you pipe down!" she snapped at the dog, then bent over and patted him to calm him down. "Oh yuck!" She looked at her hand where she had patted the dog. It did not smell bad—just very perfumey. "Oh no," she sighed. She looked at the twins. A sign was taped to their wagon: Bu-Tee-On-Weels. Then she saw the flash of the dog's brightly painted pink toenails and saw the hair curler in its tail. It was all coming together now.

"You didn't," she said, looking up at the twins.

They nodded solemnly. "You don't understand, Zanny."

"No, I guess I don't," she said with patience.

Zanny Duggan had infinite patience. That was what made her such a good fourth-grade teacher. She was the daughter of Rosemarie Duggan, the production manager of Starbuck Recital Wear, and she had babysat all the Starbuck children over the years. All the kids loved her. And she loved them.

"So tell me about this, girls," she said, scratching gently at the dog's throat.

"Well, we tried to get a girl to do our beauty on, but Felicity Farnham said no. So she said we could do her dog," Charly began.

"Oh, dear!" Zanny sighed with relief and rolled her

eyes toward heaven, thankful that Felicity Farnham was spared the beauty.

"Do you know that if Dad takes that job in London, Aunt Honey is going to take care of us?" Molly asked.

"I'd heard that rumor, yes."

"Well, do you want that to happen?" Charly shoved her face with its runny nose right up to Zanny's. Her little cowlicks stuck out, rigid with mousse, and her bright blue eyes were wide and unblinking.

"Well, of course not. No, I can see the problem."

"There's no problem if we don't go to London. If we make money, Dad won't have to go to work . . ."

"Oh, no!" Zanny spoke softly but slapped her own cheek in disbelief. She did love five-year-olds. She did, indeed. Even little Sammy Kendall had been okay when he was five. But now they had just decided to hold him back a year, which meant he would repeat fourth grade, and Jane Gerstein wasn't up to him again, so that could mean both Sammy and Randy in her classroom, and—oh gosh, London did sound good!

That evening the light of an almost full spring moon streamed through both the curved windows in the twin turrets of the older children's bedrooms. In J. B.'s room, illuminated by the moon's light, the head of Sherlock Holmes cast a jagged shadow. It stretched right up the walls and covered the ceiling above the bed where J. B. slept. And in Liberty's room, although there was no shadow of Sherlock, deep within her dark sleep, something silvery splashed against her dream—a distant echo from another world, another time.

5

True, False, or Plastic—Whatever Happened to Baker Street?

THEY HAD ONLY BEEN in London a day, but Zanny had promised to take them to Baker Street as soon as possible so they could try and find Number 221B, where Sherlock and Dr. Watson, his partner in solving crimes, had lived. Now Liberty and July felt a queasy feeling way down deep in their stomachs.

It was like a bad dream. As they came up the escalator from the subway, or the underground, as Londoners called it, the tiled walls of the Baker Street stop seemed to explode with craggy silhouettes of Sherlock Holmes—each tile bore the famous profile complete with the deerstalker cap and the Meerschaum pipe jammed between his teeth. It wasn't like seeing double, it was like seeing in multiples squared. Everywhere the profile, until they finally emerged into the glaring light of Baker Street.

There was a pub called Moriarty's, after the evil genius who was Holmes's archenemy. There was even a Sherlock Holmes hotel, all modern and ugly, made of glass and chrome. The hotel boasted a Watson Room, and almost next door was an Italian Ristorante Moriarty. Just about every corner boasted a souvenir shop hawking key chains, mugs, placemats, soap, and even candy sporting pictures of Sherlock. Postcards and posters, pens and pencil cases, napkins and T-shirts were all for sale. It was impossible to escape the profile, for it had been emblazoned on every surface where one walked or looked, on every item one might buy. Quotes from the tales had been inscribed over doorways of pubs, restaurants, and shops.

It's almost like graffiti, Liberty flashed as she spotted yet another profile of Holmes. This one was above the entrance to a chemist's shop.

Like? Is! July flashed back.

Well, after all, he's just a character in a novel.

What do you mean, just a character in a novel—that's not graffiti!

July found Liberty's attitude annoying. Liberty herself knew in a microflash that what she had said wasn't true at all, and she regretted it almost immediately. Sherlock Holmes was a character. In many ways he was more famous than his creator, Sir Arthur Conan Doyle. That meant something. She wasn't sure *what* it meant, but she knew it didn't mean this kind of cheap, plastic exploitation.

"Well, kids," Zanny said with pluck, "let's find Number 221B, Baker Street." She sensed their disappointment. All the buildings appeared decidedly modern with their glass-and-concrete exteriors, hardly the dark old Victorian London in the books. They stood before a dry-cleaning store with a sign that said "Sherlock Holmes would have used our services."

"221B," July said. "That is the exact address. But this guidebook here says that there never was any 221B, and the actual address is probably the present-day Number 31."

"Well, here we are at Number 50, so we must be near," Zanny said.

They crossed the street to a block of rather ugly modern concrete buildings. And, in fact, a small oval plaque bearing the profile of Holmes was on the front of one building. It stated that this was where the fictional detective's rooms would have been if he had actually ever lived at the address 221B in Victorian London.

July and Liberty tried to imagine a narrow old building with a tall brick chimney. They envisioned the rooms that Holmes and Dr. Watson had rented, the rooms in which they sat and figured out the solutions to the great crimes of the century. They tried to imagine Holmes's study, the tick of the clock, the glowing embers in the grate of the fireplace, the solitary pool of light from his reading lamp, the smoke curling from his pipe as Sherlock, the greatest detective ever, contemplated a case. They had known it was fiction, that it wasn't really true, but did it have to be this false, this plastic?

Charly's little voice piped up. "This is where that

guy lived? This is boring. Disney World would have done it better!"

"Hush, Charly," Zanny said.

But July and Liberty didn't even care. Charly was right. Disney would have done it better.

The Starbucks had found a small hotel in Marylebone that was favored as a way station for newly arrived embassy families looking for more permanent residences. It was ideal as far as the children were concerned. Regent's Park, a wonderful place, was two blocks away. Baker Street was two blocks in the opposite direction. Madame Tussaud's, the famous waxworks, was a mere ten-minute walk from the hotel. All kinds of restaurants and movie theaters and even a McDonald's—thank goodness!—were nearby. None of the twins was particularly excited by English cuisine.

"Bangers!" muttered Charly, staring at a fat grilled sausage on her plate. After the disappointment of Baker Street, the children had been so hungry they stopped for lunch in a pub.

"Shepherd's pie! I thought it would be quiche," Liberty whispered. "This looks like mystery meat, and what is that on the side, Zanny?"

"Potatoes."

"They're so gray looking," July said. "They look more like oatmeal than potatoes."

"Dust pussies," Molly said. "They look just like those dust pussies Mom slurps up with the hand vacuum behind the couch."

"Oh gross!" said all the twins.

"Hush! All of you. That is not the least bit polite. You cannot be so narrow." Zanny looked at them sharply. "We can go to McDonald's in Washington, but we're in London, now. It's time we broadened our horizons, not to mention our tastes. We are here to learn about a new culture." She looked carefully at all four children. Zanny had curly reddish blonde hair, the color of an apricot, and a face full of copper freckles. Her eyes were a bright cornflower blue. "Remember our deal?" she said, raising a finger.

"No school, right?" said Charly.

"Not if we can help it." Zanny smiled.

The children and Zanny had hatched a plan to avoid school for the whole year.

Why go to an American school in London, July had asked on the plane trip over. If Mom thinks living in London would be such a wonderful learning experience, why not also go to an English school?

It turned out that enrolling any of the children in a conveniently located English school would be difficult. And then Zanny, who basically agreed with July, had come up with the notion that she should be the children's teacher. After all, she had just quit her job teaching in a Chevy Chase elementary school. She had decided to take a break. Maybe she would go back to grad school. Maybe she would teach again in a year or two. But for now, why not have a home school with the Starbuck children? The only difference would be that the curriculum would be the city of London and English history.

Put thought it sounded appealing. Madeline was less certain. They would mull it over during the summer.

The kids thought it sounded fantastic. They loved Zanny. They knew they could always trust her and that Zanny did not always follow parental rules. However, that night July and Liberty would break a rule that they knew would stretch even Zanny's understanding. But it was too tempting, and those strange echoes kept thrumming in their heads—those echoes of a voice that perhaps knew no rules. And that gave them courage.

In the hotel, Liberty shared a bedroom with Zanny. July was in a connecting room. They had all been sound asleep for hours, but something had stirred Liberty's sleep long before dawn. She turned over and pulled the covers up around her neck. At first she thought she was having a dream about sand, for there was a dry, whispery sound, but then the sound of the sand turned to that of silvery rain, then sand again. No, perhaps a fine drizzle? Sand, rain, wind, a storm of tiny particles bombarded her dreamless sleep, and at the eye of the storm . . . were there more than the whispered weathery sounds? Were there smeared words, muffled voices?

"This is not a dream!"

Liberty sat bolt upright. There was no mystery

about that voice. She knew immediately her own voice had spoken those five words. And the words had come straight out of her mouth, not her mind, not teleflashed to or from her brother. Good grief, she could have wakened Zanny.

She looked over at the other bed. Zanny slept on, undisturbed by Liberty's outburst. She looks pretty when she sleeps, Liberty thought. Her hair was all frizzy and golden red around her face. Liberty yawned. She had a feeling that she looked dumb when she slept. Her mouth probably hung open, and she suspected that she drooled, too, because sometimes there was a small damp spot on her pillow.

Liberty turned and looked out the window. How odd, she thought. It was so light out, too light for the time: two o'clock in the morning. And yet she couldn't see the buildings across the street from the hotel. She climbed out of bed and went over to the window.

"It's fog!" she whispered to herself. It was the thickest fog she had ever seen, and it was beautiful. Streetlights wrapped in the thick vapor looked like huge, lustrous pearls.

Liberty was enchanted. Something was so magical about the fog and the night. Sherlock Holmes would walk with Watson through a fog like this. Suddenly Liberty's imagination filled with images of dark water and misty wharves and swirling fog shrouding stealthy figures that sliced through a London night.

At that very moment July appeared in the doorway, rumpled and scratching his head. "Holmes used to pick up his dog, Toby, on Pinchin Lane, right down by the river."

He yawned.

Liberty usually didn't actually wake July up with her thoughts, but this time the images in her mind had been so vivid, like beautiful and powerful paintings, that it was as if paint had spilled off her canvas onto another—her twin brother's. But that was only part of it. There was more.

She remembered those whispers from before she woke, the echoing of dreams. Not her dreams, perhaps. Other dreams. Some other voice trying to break in—but from where? And why? She bet that July's sleep had been laced by the same dim echoes. There was something oddly disturbing and, yes, invasive about it. July would understand.

Then the thought seized them both at the same time, as if the idea had been swept in by the whispering wind behind the swirling fog outside. But it was so bold, so tantalizing, so outrageous—not to mention in violation of every rule of common sense and safety—that they knew not to say it out loud.

I think we should go for a walk through the city.

Of course. To the river, to Pinchin Lane.

Where else?

It would be terribly dangerous. They knew that from the start. Two kids, alone, making their way through a strange city in dense fog. It was preposterous. Zanny would resign or get fired if she discovered they were doing it and didn't stop them. Their parents would die if they found out.

But this did not stop them. As J. B. slipped a map into his pocket, Liberty began to have the strangest feeling that something powerful, something momentous was about to happen—an adventure worthy of the great master of detection himself—Sherlock Holmes!

6

The Pinscher of Pinchin Lane

THEY STEPPED OUT into the chill midnight air. The streetlights really did hang like pearls—beautiful, huge, soft, luminous pearls swirled in veils of fog. Shapes melted into the milky night. The breath of the fog together with a faint wind seemed to stir things and change ordinary objects like street signs, hanging plants, stoplights into something slightly strange and extraordinary. It was not a night to trust the appearance of things, the familiar, the normal, or the known. It was rather a night that suggested the possibility of fantastic transformations.

The twins stood briefly on the corner of the intersection of Marylebone High Street and Nottingham. Mist swirled about them. The underground had stopped. But it didn't matter. They would walk. They were out to enjoy the fog. They set off down Marylebone in the pearly light.

Normally busy during the day, the street was now almost deserted. They headed for the Thames River, toward Pinchin Lane, home of Toby. Toby had been half spaniel, half lurcher, and Holmes had used him to trail suspects. On and on the twins walked toward the river.

They had J. B.'s map, and when the fog occasionally thinned to a point where they could read the street signs, they matched them with the names on the map.

"This must be Carlos Place," Liberty said as she passed a very fancy-looking hotel where a doorman tipped his top hat and said, "Lovely evening for a stroll."

Funny he doesn't think it's weird, two kids out all by themselves, J. B. teleflashed as the doorman replaced his top hat.

Yes, but . . .

But what?

I'm not sure. There was something in his voice kind of like—

Kind of like the echoes?

Sort of, but not really.

Who knew, Liberty thought. The evening seemed so magical. If streetlights looked like pearls, maybe she and July looked like grown-ups in the thick fog.

Carlos Place led to Mount Street, and two right turns brought them to Curzon. Two cats melted out of the mist, their yellow eyes blazing like gold nuggets. Down Half Moon Street the children went. Then they crossed Piccadilly.

"This must be the park," Liberty said.

"Which one?" asked J. B.

"Let's look." She unfolded the map. "It's Green Park."

"Wish I'd brought my skateboard," J. B. muttered as they trotted along a narrow footpath.

"What's that?" Liberty stopped in her tracks. Ahead in the fog loomed an immense shape. The strange swirling mists seemed to obliterate the edges of things, contours as well as boundaries. When Liberty looked up she felt the crushing presence of a shape that might tumble right down on her.

"Oh," she said with a sigh of relief. And they walked right up to the base of the pedestal.

"Queen Victoria." In order to read the letters, July had to practically put his nose against the bronze plaque.

"And it's over eighty feet tall," Liberty added. "I read that in a guide. And now I remember that if she's here, St. James's Park must be right over there." Liberty pointed a finger into the fog. July looked and shook his head. The tip of her finger seemed to dissolve in the mist. "And," continued Liberty, "that'll be the most direct way to the river. You say Pinchin Lane is right near Westminster Bridge, J. B.?"

"Yes."

"This is the oldest of the royal parks in London."

"You got that from the guide, too?"

"No, that was Zanny, part of our English curriculum—the one that's going to save us from going to regular school. You've got to take it more seriously, July. If we really pay attention to Zanny, believe me,

Mom and Dad will forget about our going to that school they called up."

"If we really paid attention to Zanny we wouldn't be doing this right now!"

The truth of J. B.'s remark was so overwhelmingly apparent that there was nothing else either one could say. They were both silent for a few minutes as they walked.

Are we really foolish?

Yeah, but . . .

We're out here all alone in this fog. Are you scared?

Not really.

There could be criminals lurking! Liberty thought of all the books she had been reading that talked about the thieves and pickpockets and murderers of old London. In those days, children were not just kidnapped but bought and sold like goods and worked until they were worn out. Worse still, they could be captured and mutilated and then set out to beg. Minus a finger or an eye, they would appear so pathetic that no self-respecting Englishman could walk by without tossing them a farthing. London had been known as one of the most vicious capitals in Western Europe in the last century. There was a staggering crime rate, and the streets and gin lanes teemed with professional criminals, gangs of burglars, and highwaymen. *Yikes! What are we doing out here!*

It was really your idea, Liberty. Don't go chicken on me. Look, in this fog they can't even see us.

And we can't see them!

If the criminals that might be lurking in the fog-shrouded night could not see them, July and Liberty were certainly not going to let them hear them. So, in silent agreement, the twins decided not to talk out loud until they were back safe in their rooms at the hotel. They continued walking to St. James's Park, following the path around a horse statue that reared with its rider into the fog.

Henry the Eighth built this park, Liberty flashed, trying to change the subject.

Before or after he chopped off his wife's head?

Thanks. Thanks a bunch, Jelly Bean!

Well, I just wondered. I mean, just imagine if he came up with this nice little idea for a pretty park on the same day he cut off what's-her-name's head?

Anne Boleyn.

Suddenly a powerful, sweet fragrance enveloped them. A wind had come up and pushed the scent of roses through the thickening fog.

Where is it coming from? J. B. asked. It was absolutely impossible to see anything now. The few lights in the park were just dim smears in the night.

Let's follow the scent and see if we can find the roses.

Rose hounds instead of bloodhounds.

Look, right here!

A gust of wind had made a sudden clearing in the fog just where July stood. There, a few feet ahead of Liberty, he found himself in the middle of two facing crescents of roses. The roses appeared pink and golden and peachy. Their petals were embroidered with tiny beads of mist that gave them a silvery sheen. The fragrance was almost overpowering, intoxicating.

I feel like we're breathing magic, Liberty flashed. She closed her eyes. Did she, for just a millisecond, hear an echo? Or was it the scent of roses in her head?

Liberty! You look all silvery and bright.

So do you!

They looked at each other in amazement. It was as if they had suddenly grown older. Their jet black hair was beaded with droplets of dew and now appeared as silver as their grandma's out in Kansas. But their faces were still young and freckled, and their eyes were bright.

Liberty noticed a funny expression on July's face. She had seen that smile before somewhere. It was so familiar—the mouth slightly parted in a daring half smile of anticipation. She knew. It was the smile of adventurers. She had seen it in history books in the portraits of explorers, and, yes, in the pictures of Sherlock Holmes, himself.

You're smiling, Liberty. You must be starting to enjoy yourself.

I'm smiling! Suddenly she felt as if she had been admitted to the most exclusive club in the world. Was she really looking at her mirror image? Was she a true adventurer, one who could almost smile and be afraid at the same time?

You are!

The two little words broke loose in her head, but it was not J. B. speaking. It was the echo. She knew there was no turning back now.

They went left on Birdcage Walk, which bordered the south side of the park. They had gone little more than a block when they heard chimes. One . . . two . . . three times they sounded. Suddenly the twins felt as if their own bodies had grown hollow, and the gongs were filling their very beings. There seemed to be no separation between them and the chimes. But when the ringing stopped and the last echoes had faded from their brains, the feeling left. Their bodies became their own again, and they walked straight to Westminster Bridge. In the middle, they stopped to watch the fog hovering over the river and a few faintly pulsing green and red lights on riverboats making their way up or down the river.

Christmas trees! Floating through clouds. The thought filled both the twins' minds at once.

When they reached the other side of Westminster Bridge they stood under a very dim streetlight. J. B. got out his Sherlock Holmes Mystery Map of London, a going-away present from Zanny's mother. He also took out his pocket edition of Sir Arthur Conan Doyle's *The Sign of Four*.

He pointed to the map. *If we're here ##**^&*

*What? %#@@****

It was unbelievable! The twins' communication was breaking up. This rarely happened and certainly never in these circumstances. They had experienced static before, like when their father had made the visit to their school for the War on Fluorocarbons, or once when they had been on a car trip and driven along a stretch of highway where there were massive electrical transformers, but that wasn't the case here at all. They had just crossed the Thames and were standing on what looked like a very small, quiet street.

Liberty tried again:

**&#####++

%%%!!###&&

It was impossible. Their telepathic channels had been invaded. But it was not the echo. No, when the echo came, it came gently with a soft, wind-whispery song. This was pure scratchy static, like the sound of fingernails on a blackboard, and it made them shiver.

"It's awful!" Liberty blurted out.

"Hush! If we have to talk out loud we can at least whisper." July shook out the map. "Look, we need to figure out where we are. There should be a hospital around here someplace."

"What do you call that?" Liberty said, pointing to a large red and white building directly in front of them.

"Do you think that's a hospital?" J. B. asked.

"Well, it's certainly too big for a house."

They walked closer. They saw the emergency sign before they saw the one that said St. Thomas's Hospital.

"Okay, aha!" exclaimed J. B. "The game is afoot!"

July seemed to have forgotten completely that their ability to telecommunicate had been totally interrupted. Doesn't he care? wondered Liberty. She herself felt as if her arm or leg had been amputated.

"Shoot! I should have remembered to wear my Sherlock Holmes hat! Can you believe it?"

No, she couldn't believe it. Here she was worried, mortally worried, about the loss of something she could never remember being without, and there was July, worried about his stupid deerstalker hat! He was fuming.

"I'm finally out of Washington, D.C., in London, England, actually retracing Dr. Watson's steps in *The Sign of Four*, and I forget to wear my hat."

"July, how can you be worrying about your hat? Don't you realize what has happened to us?" Liberty was speaking in a whisper that quickly became a rasp of desperation.

"What are you talking about?" He looked up, his gray eyes blank. There was no recognizable glimmer in those eyes. It had been a night of strange transformations already, but this was the most terrifying of any imaginable. Was her own twin brother becoming a stranger?

"J. B., don't you care?"

"Care about what?"

"The static, our telepathy. What will we do without it?"

"You have to learn to adapt."

"What?" This was unbelievable. Something was taking over J. B. He looked the same and yet—"J. B., I can't believe it. We've always been telepathic."

"It's not going to kill us to have to talk out loud."

Liberty was beyond dismay. And who knew, it just might kill them. Hadn't they agreed in the park to talk silently because of all the criminals?

"July, it's a part of us. How would you feel if somebody came up and said, 'We'll just amputate your little toe here, it won't kill you'?"

"Little toe." He looked up vacantly from the map. Then he looked down again.

"Okay," J. B. said, giving the map a snap. "I can deduct that if this building here is St. Thomas's Hospital, then if we turn right we enter a section called Lambeth. And if we follow Doyle's directions . . . Here, I've got it marked."

It was useless. Maybe this change in July and the interruption of the telepathic channels was temporary. She'd better just go along with him. "Read Doyle's directions," Liberty said in a weary voice.

"Just a minute." J. B. turned the pages rapidly in the book. "Okay. Here we go." He began to read from the story:

" 'Pinchin Lane was a row of shabby two-storied brick houses in the lower quarter of Lambeth. I had to knock for some time at No. 3 before I could make any impression. At last, however, there was a glint of a candle behind the blind, and a face looked out at the upper window.'

" ' "Go on, you drunken vagabond," said the face. "If you kick up any more row, I'll open the kennels and let out forty-three dogs upon you." ' "

July stopped reading. "But now, over here on the next page, it says, ' "Toby lives at No. 7, on the left here." He moved slowly forward with his candle among the queer animal family which he had gathered round him.' Remember that part, Liberty? I always thought it was so spooky."

"You mean the guy who keeps Holmes's dogs?" Liberty felt a glimmer of hope. July seemed a little bit more like himself. Maybe if she just kept him talking about all this he would get back to normal.

"Yeah, that guy. Remember? He had a sort of kennel. But not just dogs. Listen to this." July hunched over the book and continued to read: " 'In the uncertain, shadowy light I could see dimly that there were glancing, glimmering eyes peeping down at us from every cranny and corner. Even the rafters above us were lined by solemn fowls, who lazily shifted their weight from one leg to the other as our voices disturbed their slumbers.' "

"Oooh, creepy!" Liberty said. "I hope we don't see any animals. I'm really not big on animals, especially small, creepy, vicious ones."

"Come on!" J. B. urged. "We have to get to the lower quarter of Lambeth."

They turned down an alley behind one of the hospital buildings that seemed to lead in the direction of lower Lambeth. One dumpster warned of toxic waste materials. Something scurried under a fence and banged against an empty metal drum. Dark squarish shapes loomed out of the fog—containers for the disposables, the trash of a hospital. It was not pleasant to think about the trash of a hospital and what might be in those containers. Suddenly a brighter light melted the fog around them.

"Quick, against the wall!" July hissed and grabbed Liberty's hand. "I don't think we should be here." Even his hand felt a little different. Was this really her twin? A strange unknowable feeling seemed to invade her body. For the first time she felt very separate and disconnected, very single.

It was such an odd feeling that she almost reeled from it; losing gravity would not have felt any stranger and would have probably been a lot more fun. This was awful. It was profoundly sad to have this feeling of separateness when the hand that held hers was genetically, down to the last molecule, the closest and most identical to her own in the entire universe. In that one split second Liberty realized she was feeling an emotion she had never experienced in her life—loneliness. She felt as if she were standing on the rim of the blackest, deepest abyss. This may be worse than death, she thought.

Where have you gone, J. B.? My old Jelly Bean, where have you gone? There was only silence from July, and although there was no static, Liberty could sense that her own flashes had grown dim like the embers of a dying fire.

A very long car swung into the alley. Two attendants jumped out to open the rear door.

"Hello, mate!" a voice called out cheerfully. "Got one here for you for Heathrow Airport. Bound for sunny Spain. The six A.M. flight. Not the way I'd want to go, mind you, though me wife and I been saving our pennies for a trip."

Two white-coated people came out of a garage door carrying a stretcher. On the stretcher, a lumpy form was draped with a sheet. The cover blew slightly in the wind. Liberty squeezed her eyes shut. What if the wind blew so hard that she saw a hand, a dead man's hand?

When the hearse pulled away with its cargo, they came out from the press of foggy night shadows and crept down the alley. Here the alleyways never seemed to run straight for more than a few yards at a time; they twisted and turned and became as crooked as a dog's hind legs. There were no longer simple rows of shabby two-storied brick houses. A few were left, but most had been torn down.

It appeared that the sprawling hospital complex had gobbled up much of the area. Many of the alleys and lanes remained unmarked. So it was very possible that Pinchin Lane might have lost its street sign. After all, Doyle had written *The Sign of Four* nearly a hundred years ago, and streets and neighborhoods, even in London, could change over the course of a century. That was what J. B. was thinking. Just their luck to find a McDonald's. Or worse yet, suppose the lane was still there, and someone had opened up a souvenir shop with Toby key chains and Toby T-shirts and Toby chocolate bars. Oh dear, he thought. He hoped it would not turn out to be like Baker Street.

Liberty's thoughts were following a different path altogether. She couldn't get the dead body out of her mind. Every lumpy heap, and there were several, was another corpse waiting for a trip to the morgue or Spain. And every whisper of the wind brought the sound of scurrying feet and the dread of small slithery creatures and their yellow eyes. On the creepiness scale, this was a solid ten. But worse than that, she could not get used to this strange new feeling of separateness, of being a singleton. It just *had* to be temporary.

"This is it!" July said softly.

"What?" Liberty asked.

"This must be Pinchin Lane!" July said, not concealing the delight in his voice.

It was a narrow little lane. They stood in front of an iron gate and peered through. No dustbins were visible. In the fog it appeared that there were several small buildings that could have been houses, row houses. Perhaps, July was thinking, things had not changed that much from the time when Sir Arthur Conan Doyle had written *The Sign of Four*. Then suddenly, from behind, they heard a low growl. A horrible bark rent the fog, bloodcurdling, full of fever and rage. The children screamed. The echoes that had been haunting them from Washington to London pressed in even closer, growing to a dull roar.

Instantly the current of thought between July and

Liberty became charged, sizzling with a barrage of strange, incomprehensible signals as they dashed across the street.

"It bit me. It bit me!" screeched Liberty. "My cheek! My cheek!"

It's okay, it's okay. There's no blood, Liberty.

What? Are you back, July?

I've always been right here. He paused. *Haven't I?*

Oh, Jelly Bean!

7

Number 3, Devonshire Mews

THERE WAS ONLY a scrawl of thin white foam across Liberty's cheek. And across the alley an immense dog, a Doberman pinscher, thrashed madly against its chain as it tried to leap through the fence. Its head hung between the bars. Its mouth was open and frothing foam. Its eyes were narrow green slits in the night.

"Git out! Git out!" Above the mad barking, a voice seared the night. "I got worse than that up here. I have a wiper in this bag, and I'll drop it on your 'ead. . . ."

Too frightened to scream, the twins took off. July remembered the strange speech defect of the kennel keeper in *The Sign of Four*: the *w*'s for *v*'s—"wipers" for "vipers." Liberty felt her heart pounding. As she ran, she felt the scrawl of dog spittle flatten against her cheek. A horrible cackle mixed with the baying of the Doberman. Liberty was so scared, and her heart was beating so hard, she wondered if it could burst. But it wasn't just fear—she was happy, wildly happy.

Her mouth parted slightly in that daring half smile of the adventurer, and she felt the damp mist on her lips. She was no longer a singleton. The air between Liberty and her twin crackled.

Take a left here!

Now a right, right?

Correct!

The twins ran back, threading their way through a maze of alleys and hospital buildings. They passed the place where the hearse had come to meet the dead person bound for Spain. They sprinted across Westminster Bridge. They did not even notice that the fog had begun to lift, and the tracery of the old clock now shone through thin, scudding clouds. July was the first one to falter. He clutched his ribs.

I've got a terrible stitch in my side. I have to stop.

They had stopped on the far side of the bridge just under Big Ben. The old clock began to peal the hour—thrrrinngg . . . thrrrinng . . . thrrinngg . . . thrinnnggg.

Again the twins felt themselves filled with the chimes of the dawn. The cackle and barks faded away, becoming as dim as footprints on a sandy beach when the tide rolls in.

Liberty gasped, trying to catch her breath. *What happened to Toby, the nice half-spaniel? He seems to have turned into the hound of the Baskervilles.* The color in her cheeks was high. She began to laugh.

I don't know! Boy, can you imagine what Mom and Dad and Zanny would do if they found out about all this!

Forget it! Liberty flashed. She touched her face where the dog's spittle had been. She was wondering if July was really aware of what had happened. He seemed to have forgotten all about the invasion of their telepathic channels.

What's that, Liberty?

You don't remember, do you?

Remember what?

How it all broke up for us right before we got to Pinchin Lane.

What broke up?

Our communication, our telepathy.

I don't believe you. You're kidding.

No.

But we agreed to only teleflash. That's all we've been doing, right?

Wrong. The channels were invaded. It was all static and then nothing.

Nothing? July's eyes widened with horror.

You didn't feel alone?

What do you mean, Liberty?

All separate.

Separate? You mean like a singleton? Oh gosh! Gee! You mean you felt that way?

Liberty nodded solemnly. A tear began to roll down her cheek. J. B. reached out his hand.

You crossed over. It was a statement, not a question. Liberty knew what July meant. She had briefly inhabited this world alone, totally alone, as no two twins have ever done. For although twins can be in two different physical places, there is never a sense of separation. "Crossed over" was a good and a bad way to put it. She had, after all, not willfully crossed over. It was more as if she had been abandoned, left behind, and to her, the more pressing question was this: Where had July gone when he had left her behind? He now acted as if he had amnesia. He simply did not recall the invasion of their telepathic channels at all.

Was it the echoes again? Is that what caused the breakup?

Oh, no. The echoes aren't so bad. This was different. Like I said, all static and then nothing. No echoes, no whispers . . . nothing.

J. B. bit his lip lightly in concentration.

Do you remember what the person yelled out the window?

Of course. About the "wiper," dropping it on our heads. Liberty remembered too well.

J. B. looked at Liberty. Fear filled his luminous gray eyes.

Something really weird is happening. I mean, when you tell me first of all that our channels were invaded . . .

Yeah, what does that have to do with what the man yelled?

Liberty, those were the exact words that the man in the book yelled out the window to Watson when he went to get the dog. They are right there in the book.

No! Liberty flashed in disbelief.

I'll show you. July pulled the paperback out of his jacket. *I just hadn't read it to you before because I knew it would really scare you. You hate snakes so much.*

He turned quickly to the page. Under a streetlight at the north end of Westminster Bridge the twins read the passage. The words were identical to the ones that had crackled through the night on Pinchin Lane. " 'I have a wiper in this bag, and I'll drop it on your 'ead if you don't hook it!' " July and Liberty looked up at one another.

What in the world is going on?

This can't just be chance.

No way.

The odds were improbable, more than improbable, virtually impossible! Those few words out of all the billions, trillions of words in the English language—the very same words as in the book, in the exact same order, with the exact same speech defect: *v* replaced by *w*, the *h* dropped from "head." Identical words tumbling out of a window on the exact same lane one hundred years later! How could it be? *The Sign of Four* had been a made-up story, and this was real life. What could be more real than Liberty and July Starbuck standing on the pavement in the thinning mist of a chilly London dawn?

So what could have happened? J. B. wondered. What could it all mean? Was there some Sherlock Holmes scholar tucked away on Pinchin Lane living out the life of the kennel keeper? And what about

Toby? Had he indeed been transformed into that baleful Doberman pinscher?

They walked the rest of the way back quietly, following the path once more around St. James's Park. The gilt-tipped black gates of Buckingham Palace gleamed in the pink-gray morning light. Above the roof the Royal Standard flew, indicating the queen was in residence. And just inside the courtyard they could see the guards in front of the guardhouses in their towering bearskin hats and scarlet tunics glistening with bright brass buttons and badges.

They took a slanting path across Green Park to Piccadilly. The city was just waking up, and in Mayfair a few housemaids and manservants were out washing down white marble steps that led up to cream-colored houses. Soon they crossed Oxford Street and lingered in front of a display window of a department store that showed disco wear.

As a city wakes, each sound comes separately and distinctly, and even the most common sound acquires a certain grace of its own at that early hour. The creaking of a lorry, or truck, as it rounds a corner, the gasp of a bus exhaling its fumes, the crank of an awning lowered by a shopkeeper, the sound of keys in a doorway, or the thwap of a newspaper tossed on a step; all of these sounds had a cozy distinction. But within an hour, they would blur into the white noise of a city fully awake.

The twins had thought they had entered Marylebone through the same route they had followed hours earlier. But indeed they had crossed Oxford Street one block to the east and had somehow gone too far. Before they knew it, they found themselves on Wimpole Street. For some reason, J. B. and Liberty felt almost unconsciously drawn to that street. It was charming.

Narrow, elegant, and immaculately kept, the houses were built out of a variety of materials—some brick, some a deep ruddy pink sandstone, some a dark charcoal gray. Each entryway was unique and special in some small way. One house had an elaborately carved dark wooden door, oiled and polished to a deep luster. Another house had a gleaming black door, and its front steps were a black-and-white checkerboard pattern of marble. At the top of the street was Devonshire Place. Inexplicably the two children, without saying a word, turned right and then right again. They followed a crooked little alley. But this one was not dark, nor was it filled with dustbins. It widened into a broader courtyard.

I think this is what they call a mews, Liberty flashed.

What's a mews?

Kind of a small, hideaway street behind a bigger street, where they've turned the old stables into houses.

Stables?

Yeah, you know, from the olden times. These were the stables for the big houses on the big street. These backed right up to them. Aren't they cute?

July had to agree. Almost like small painted dollhouses, each one was a different ice-cream color. One was pale pink, another soft green with bright yellow flowers cascading gaily down from window boxes. Another was peach, and yet another was dazzling white with a spray of morning glories just opening against its freshly whitewashed walls. But it was the plain one at the end with unpainted charcoal gray brick and varnished wooden doors that drew their attention.

It almost beckoned them with an invisible finger. A big copper tub, as brightly polished as the sparkling brass work of the front doorknob and knocker, gleamed in the morning sun. A riot of orange and yellow nasturtiums exploded softly over its edges.

This is it, the twins both thought in unison. What *it* exactly was they were not sure.

There was a rental sign in the window with a phone number.

Well, we should live here, flashed Liberty.

Of course!

Of course!

I'm not sure why.

Me *neither.*

But this place is for us. Can't you just tell?

Yes.

Who said that? Liberty flashed.

Who said what? asked July.

Who said yes? she repeated.

I thought it was you, Liberty.

It wasn't me, Liberty said. *But you heard it, too?*
Yes.

Yes!

There it is again! both twins flashed, their words seeming to collide in midair.

It's like the word "chop" back in Washington, the day Aunt Honey came for dinner, the way that word just popped up. I mean, it popped up in my head, but it was like an echo.

July nodded. *It's like this other voice is always trying to break in, listening to us.*

Whispering to us . . .

We should remember this phone number on the sign and give it to Mom and Dad. They might want to look at this place. It might be a nice place to live.

They both concentrated on memorizing the phone number: 01-453-9292.

01-453-9292
01-453-9292

01-453-9292

July and Liberty's eyes opened wide. They had each repeated the numbers once. One and one added up to two—not three. But they had both heard it again. And it was not quite an echo, because if it had been an echo of their telepathic transmission, there would have been two echoes, one for each voice.

Yes? Liberty flashed tentatively.

Yes? July flashed back.

Yes.

They turned their heads as if looking for someone, another person. This time they knew it was no echo. A clear, soft voice had just spoken. A voice that only the twins could hear.

8

Twerps, Tantrums, and Twins

CHARLY AND MOLLY were not taking to the English curriculum with quite the zest Zanny had hoped they would. At this very moment, in fact, they were playing their favorite game: Ranch. Ranch was a distinctly American game. Basically, they found something they could straddle—a footstool or a sturdy carton—and pretended they were riding their horses around the ranch wearing, of course, their Davy Crockett coonskin caps, which to them were fine substitutes for cowboy hats. They loved the coonskin caps more than anything and had screamed bloody murder when their father had suggested they leave them back in the United States.

Liberty and July hated to hear them play Ranch, especially now when they were so tired. They had crept back into the hotel apartment just in time for breakfast. July had gone back down to get the newspaper as he did every morning. Today, however, the twins had turned to the real estate section, and there was the house in the mews with the same phone number listed that they had memorized! They placed the newspaper folded open to this spot at their father's place. There was no way Putnam could miss the ad, and he said it looked promising. He left immediately after breakfast to look at the house.

As tired as Liberty and July were, sleep proved impossible with the Ranch racket going on. Not only were the younger twins noisy when they played Ranch, but they yelled at their make-believe horses in very severe voices. They were into "horsey discipline" as Madeline called it. But their mother dismissed it as an understandable part of being the youngest family members and needing to boss someone, even an imaginary horse. They actually had three horses: Rancher, Fred, and Cherry Garcia. The third horse was named for their father's favorite ice-cream flavor. Zanny now stood scowling in the doorway of the living-room suite, where Charly and Molly were straddling two large suitcases. A third suitcase was tied with a curtain cord to a nearby end table.

"You're a very naughty horse, Cherry!" Molly slapped and kicked the suitcase. "Come on. Stop eating. It's time to catch those cows."

"Oh, Rancher's a good boy!" cooed Charly. "Come on, Rancher, we got to go git the herd! Oh, bad Fred! Bad! Come on, Rancher, let's ride over. Fred, you're going to have to be punished."

"Oh, gee, this is sick!" July said. He was tired from his night's jaunt through the fog and did not have the patience to hear imaginary horses being scolded by his twerpy little sisters at the top of their lungs.

"You're wrecking the suitcases, kicking them like that," Zanny said.

"Not to mention those yucky runny noses of theirs dripping on them." Liberty yawned.

"Come on, children. If you come with me and do a little reading of *Peter Rabbit* . . ."

"You also said you'd make us Peter Bunny costumes," Charly interrupted.

"Not me. I don't want to be some dumb rabbit," Molly groused. "I'd rather be Jemima Puddle-duck. She gets to wear a pretty dress and a hat."

"Not a dress exactly. A scarf and a bonnet," Charly corrected.

"A shawl," Liberty said.

"Yeah." Molly nodded solemnly. "A shawl and a bonnet. I want one."

"Me, too," said Charly.

Zanny sighed, and, of course, seeing that she was tired, they struck.

"We want shawls! We want bonnets!" they chanted, kicking their imaginary steeds.

"I don't believe this!" July groaned.

"You are acting like total creeps," Liberty roared above the din.

"Twerps. Twin twerps having tantrums!" July said.

"You're being very immature, girls," Zanny said evenly through clenched teeth.

"Immature!" J. B. exclaimed. "They are being premature, prenatal, nonhuman!"

The twins began to dance madly around their older brother. They were as wild as banshees, chanting and flailing their arms about, their red hair spiking up like licks of flame. They stuck out their tongues and made faces at their brother.

"Shut up, you little sun-ripened pig droppings!" he yelled.

"Shut up yourself, you son of a motherless goat!" Charly yelled back.

"Son of a motherless goat! Son of a motherless goat!" they now began chanting.

Zanny clapped her hands together loudly. "If all of you don't settle down this instant I will not only not tell you the surprise, but—unless you improve your behavior immediately—you will not get to be part of the surprise."

The twins froze. "You mean we'll be left out?" Charly gasped.

"Precisely," said Zanny. "Left out." She said the words slowly and distinctly. "But then again, if you don't know what the surprise is, then you won't know what you're missing. So it won't matter."

"Yes it will!" Molly wiped her nose on her sleeve. "Me and Charly are always getting left out of things we don't know about."

"Yeah," nodded Charly. "And we don't like it one bit."

"If you don't know about it, how do you know you're being left out?" Liberty asked.

Such reasoning was lost on Molly and Charly. "We do know. We just do." Charly directed a withering look toward Liberty. "So what's the surprise?" she asked, turning back to Zanny.

"It's about July and Liberty's birthday." The little twins settled down immediately. They loved anything to do with birthdays.

"What about their birthday?" Molly asked.

"Your father was able to get one of the stretch limos from the embassy for the whole day to drive through the countryside or anywhere we want to go."

"You mean one of those fancy ones?" Charly asked.

"Yes, complete with snacks, television, telephone, and . . ." Zanny paused. She was saving the best for last. She knew the little twins would love this. "Light-up makeup mirrors with little counters and built-in shelves."

"Oh my goodness!" exclaimed Molly.

"Mercy!" exclaimed Charly.

Both twins were in an absolute lather of excitement. Charly and Molly loved playing with makeup even more than they loved playing Ranch. They had brought their makeup kits to England, filled with samples of stuff Aunt Honey got in the mail or picked up free in department stores, as well as their favorite gift—press-on nails. Liberty figured that between them, the little twins had enough press-on nails for two thousand fingers or a small town.

"But I am going to be loath to take such immature little girls," Zanny said, looking at them sternly.

"Oh goodie!" they both squealed. Zanny looked slightly confused as Charly and Molly began leaping about with a new chant. "We're going to the country in a stretch limo! We're going to the country in a stretch limo!"

"I said 'loath' to take you, not 'love' to take you."

The girls stopped dancing. It was their turn to look confused. "What do you mean?" Molly asked.

"Loath. The word means," Zanny spoke distinctly, "I do not want to take you if you act like immature little girls."

"Oh!" Molly and Charly said with a new soberness in their voices.

Just then Putnam and Madeline Starbuck came through the door of the hotel suite. They were smiling broadly.

"Great news!" Putnam boomed.

"You got the house in the mews!" Liberty exclaimed.

"We most certainly did!" Madeline said. "I am going to feel much better now about your being here. I really didn't want to fly back to Washington until we got you settled."

I knew it! July teleflashed.

Isn't it a little strange? But good, Liberty flashed back. They were both jumping up and down.

"When do we move in?" July asked.

"Day after tomorrow," Putnam said. "They're having a crew clean up, and we can move in the next day."

It was a festive evening. They all were thrilled about the unpainted house in the mews, trim and plain as a Quaker lady, with its varnished doors and bright copper tub spilling orange and yellow nasturtiums.

It had been a long day. For Liberty and July it had begun just after midnight.

As July walked past Charly and Molly's room he saw the little twins crouched on the floor.

"Dare you!" Molly slapped shut a very small book.

"I can look at it." Charly glared fiercely at her sister. "It doesn't scare me."

"What are you two doing in there?" July stopped at the door.

"She's scared to look at the picture," Molly said.

"What picture?" July asked.

"The picture in *Roly Poly Pudding,*" Molly said.

"It's a picture of Tom Kitten being rolled up in a piece of dough." Charly's bottom lip started to tremble.

July walked over to where the twins were. "Let's see it," he said.

Molly opened the small book. A little kitten, rigid with fear, his eyes staring wildly, not believing what was actually happening to him, had indeed been wrapped in dough and rolled into a sausage shape. Two rats were rolling this little bundle under their rolling pin. There was something grotesque about the picture. J. B. could see why Charly was scared. He felt a queasiness swim up in the back of his throat. "They're going to bake this cat into a pudding?"

"Yep." Charly sighed.

"They're making him into a dumpling first. They caught him and tied him up and smeared him with butter," Molly said.

"Yuck. That's really disgusting."

Molly was clearly satisfied that she had made an impression on her big brother. That was enough, and she forgot about daring Charly.

J. B. walked back to his own room. There had been a time, just a few years before, when July had had to dare himself to look at a picture. It was an illustration from *The Hound of the Baskervilles*, and it showed a mad dog loping through the night, his eyes rolled back so mostly the white was showing, his fangs glistening in the moonlight.

And now he remembered the dark lane of hours before, the foggy night air torn by the bloodcurdling bark of the dog, and then the words, the exact same words that Watson had heard when he had gone down to Pinchin Lane in search of Toby the half-spaniel. Something deep within him shuddered, and J. B. felt the hair on the back of his neck stand up. There had been a murder. . . . Of course! How could he have forgotten that? In *The Sign of Four* a twin had been murdered: Bartholomew Sholto, the twin brother of Thaddeus Sholto. July turned abruptly and went back to Liberty and Zanny's room. Zanny was not in bed yet but talking in the living room with his parents. Liberty was sitting up in bed writing a postcard to her friend Muriel Braverman.

"It was real," she said before July could even ask the question.

"I thought—I guess I kind of hoped it might have been a dream."

"No," said Liberty. "We were really there on Pinchin Lane. The lane was real, the dog was real, and the words—I looked them up again in *The Sign of Four*. They were exactly the same."

"And you know," July said, "the man from the window even said 'wiper' for 'viper,' just like in the story."

"Yes," whispered Liberty, and she touched her face lightly where the scrawl of the dog's spittle had marked her cheek.

9

A Gathering of Shadows

It seems as if there is a shadow, July teleflashed.

Like the elm leaves back in Washington, cool and nice, Liberty replied.

Yes, but there is no elm tree, or any tree in sight.

How do you explain it?

I don't know. It's a feeling. You can't always explain feelings.

I wonder if we'll feel it tonight when it gets dark?

It was moving day. Luggage and boxes and recently bought furniture were being carried into Number 3, Devonshire Mews. July and Liberty were communicating telepathically because the movers were all over the place, and the realtor from the company that rented the house to them was there as well. So there was no way the twins could speak out loud about the strange sensations they had been experiencing ever since they had entered the house that morning.

"Odd place for a bell rope." One of the movers, a

burly man, almost bald, paused to look at a thick rope that hung down one wall of the garden room where they were now standing.

"Oh, I believe, actually," said Mr. Moonpenny, the man from the real estate office, "that the kitchen in former times was upstairs, and where we now stand was a terrace garden, before they enclosed it, that is. If they took tea out here it would make sense to have a bell rope to summon the servants."

"Perfect sense." The burly mover nodded. Both men looked at July and Liberty, who also nodded automatically just to be polite.

Perfect sense, July flashed.

Yes, of course. I always summon my servants when I'm in the garden taking tea.

Yes, of course.

The three words echoed. Liberty's and July's eyes flew open. Neither one of them had flashed those last three words.

The other voice! they flashed in unison.

"How are the plants?" asked Madeline, coming into the garden room. "Show me what you picked out."

Madeline Starbuck had given the twins the fun job of buying plants. Now empty, the garden room appeared to be built almost entirely of sunlight, glass, and pale, rosy brick. It was a lovely, bright space.

In such a space July and Liberty felt exceedingly odd thinking of shadows. But despite freshly painted walls and abundant sunlight, the shadows trailed them throughout this house in the mews. Yet Liberty and July were the only ones who could see or feel them. There was nothing scary or heavy or depressing about these shadows, but nonetheless the older twins felt a tinge of sadness about the place.

They were not sorry they had come, however. No, Liberty and July felt absolutely at home in Number 3, Devonshire Mews. It felt perfectly right. And the shadows, despite this tinge of sadness, reminded them of the cool shade of the elm tree back on Dakota Street. Perhaps if the shadows could be explained, their own feelings would become clearer. Both sensed that they had been brought to Number 3 for some reason.

The garden room was particularly nice. Among the plants the twins had chosen was a white jasmine guaranteed, according to the lady at the flower shop, to climb a wall, sprawl, and spread its wonderful, sweet fragrance through a room. It already had several runners two or three feet long, and the twins planned to thread it through the pale green lattice trellises that arched against the north wall. They imagined a wall of white blossoms hanging from the trellis work.

Opposite the trellises at the other end of the garden room, the wall curved into an alcove, and the floor in the alcove dropped away to a small tiled pool. Charly and Molly were busily scrubbing it out. They planned to fill it with water. Zanny had promised to take them to buy fish and perhaps even a water lily or two; the lady at the flower shop had said she could get some.

But the loveliest part of the garden room was the ceiling. All around the edges of the ceiling, someone had painted garlands of climbing roses and ivy.

Madeline Starbuck came through the garden room again. This time she was followed by Putnam's secretary from the embassy, Mrs. Rhodes. They were carrying wicker furniture. "Look what we found at—now what do you call it again, Lucille?" she said, turning to the woman.

"A jumble sale," Lucille Rhodes said.

"Yes, a jumble sale. It's the same as a rummage sale. They're having one at the church down on the corner, and we found these two wicker rockers and a lovely table. The table isn't in as good shape. But we'll put a tablecloth on top of it with a long skirt, and the handyman at the embassy can cut us a piece of glass for the top." Madeline put down the chair she was carrying and turned around. "Oooh, look! Bleeding hearts," Madeline said, spying three small pots on the windowsill.

The pink heart-shaped blossoms had dark red centers that seemed to drip like blood, and despite the similarity to a wounded heart, they were rather happy-looking flowers.

"They will look so nice on the table, especially with a pink tablecloth! Oh, this room is going to be just lovely." Madeline clasped her hands and smiled. "Warm all winter with the southern exposure and the heat from the kitchen. I'll bet you'll be able to eat out here. And Charly and Molly—you're doing such a good job on the fish pond. It will be a vision of sunlight and goldfish and bleeding hearts shot through with the scent of jasmine."

And shadows.

The two words were not spoken, but they flashed darkly through the sunlit room.

That evening shadows began to gather and darken at dinnertime, and by bedtime they were indeed a presence, but only to Liberty and July. No one else seemed aware. Still, they were not threatening or frightening in any way. And although they were thick and deep, they were never oppressive.

Liberty and July slept in the attic. It was really one room partially divided by a storage unit with drawers and shelves. The unit came out halfway across the floor from one wall. There was a bed on either side of this partition. The children could see over the unit, and both the shelves and the drawers could be opened from either Liberty's or July's side of the bedroom. Coming out from the wall opposite the unit was a tall bookcase. But in the middle of the bookcase, some shelves had been replaced by a large desktop. This desk could be shared by simply drawing up a chair from either July's side of the attic or Liberty's.

It was a wonderful room, and now July and Liberty were finishing off their quarters, doing the one thing that the architects had not done, which was to divide the desk so that two people's messes would not get mixed up. July put a piece of masking tape down the center. Then they sat facing each other across the masking-tape line.

Both twins could feel the shadows in the corners of the attic. Liberty stared at the tape. It looked dull against the light wood of the desk. "I've got an idea," she said suddenly. She went to a carton filled with her junk. "I know I put them here someplace. I just know it."

"What?"

"Ah ha! Here they are." She drew out a bag of M&M's and brought them back to the desk. She tore open the bag. "We need a little color here," she declared and began lining up the M&M's along the tape.

"Good idea," July said, helping her.

A new kind of speckled band.

The thought slithered through the air of the attic room with all the serpentine grace of the deadly swamp adder in "The Adventure of the Speckled Band." Both twins now recalled the frightening Sherlock Holmes story in which a wrathful man had killed one of his stepdaughters by training a deadly snake to crawl through a ventilator and down a bell rope that hung over her bed. The girl had died a horrible death while crying out with her last breath, "It was the band! The speckled band!" No one had known what she had meant. Until, of course, Sherlock Holmes arrived and discovered that the speckled band was the venomous snake.

Do you remember that bell rope downstairs in the garden room, the one the man said was in an odd place for a bell rope? Liberty flashed.

Yeah, but . . . July's thoughts dwindled off. It seemed weird now that they had just hours before made jokes about that bell rope. At the time he hadn't even thought of "The Adventure of the Speckled Band." *Are you scared?*

No, not really scared. Liberty put a bright yellow M&M on the tape. *It's nothing like the way I felt when we were on Pinchin Lane. But there is something happening here, July. Don't you feel we're very close to the center of it? Those funny echoes, the other voice.*

But I'm not really hearing it right now.

Maybe we're too close.

What do you mean, too close?

Maybe we're at the very source of the echo, where it comes from. So maybe it's not just an echo now. Maybe this is it, and we'll hear the first, the original sound if we listen carefully. Liberty paused for a moment in her thoughts. *Don't you wonder why we were brought here?*

Yes. Brought. We were brought, weren't we? It wasn't like we just came here.

No. Not at all. We were summoned, like the servants were summoned with the bell rope.

Called.

Convened.

Signaled.

A flock of synonyms beat on silent wings through the air, confirming one simple thing. The children were not here by accident, but by design. This very room seemed in some peculiar way to be at the center of mysterious events that reached further back than just Pinchin Lane, perhaps to when they had first begun to hear those strange echoes bouncing through their telepathic channels all the way back in Washington. Nothing appeared to be an accident or a coincidence now; everything happened on purpose. What the exact purpose or design was they could not be sure. But that their destiny was to discover its meaning, to lighten the shadows—of this they had no doubt.

Outside the two dormer windows in the gables of the attic, the soft glow of a streetlight burnished the copper tub. The nasturtiums danced in the wind like licks of flame, casting quick shadows on the paving stones. Real shadows mixed with phantom ones until they became indistinguishable from one another. All of these shadows gathered about Liberty and July as they climbed into their beds that night. A sliver of new moon hung in one of the windowpanes. They were glad to have no real walls between them, between their ends of the attic room. The shadows as well as the moonlight and starlight could be shared, could flow between them from one end of the attic to the other. July and Liberty could each be alone, and yet this cord of silver light and dancing shadows connected them whenever they wanted.

They were both growing sleepy, each twin with separate thoughts now. Liberty was thinking of why the darkness did not scare her. The opposite of light was not, after all, darkness. Weren't they in one sense both part of something else, both part of the same thing? Not just the earth and the fact that when it was night in one place it was day in another. Wasn't there really more to it than that? Didn't it go beyond just the earth? Day and night, lightness and darkness—wasn't it all like a kind of skin of the universe? It was all one skin. That was it. Yes. But could there be other universes? She yawned and fell asleep.

July's brain meanwhile had been swirling with words, fragments of sentences, paragraphs from stories of Sherlock Holmes he had read. The terrible voice on Pinchin Lane had dissolved into the night. But other parts of stories loomed. Like shards of light, these story fragments would fiercely blast through and then be swallowed by the darkness. But one story in particular threaded its words through the attic night. It was "The Adventure of the Speckled Band." July could hear Holmes's voice now, the words he had muttered in the story: "Where does that bell communicate with?" Sherlock was speaking about the bell rope that hung by the ventilator in the chamber of the murdered young woman. He had continued, "What a fool a builder must be to open a ventilator into another room, when, with the same trouble, he might have communicated with the outside air!

"Dummy bell-ropes, and ventilators which do not ventilate . . . ," Holmes had wondered aloud.

Whole pieces of conversation from the story came back to July now like a distant echo but as clearly as if the book were right before his eyes.

"I have always, about three in the morning, heard a low, clear whistle." These were the words of Julia Stoner, the murdered sister, a few nights before her death. "I cannot tell where it came from—perhaps from the next room . . ."

"I could not sleep that night," Helen Stoner, Julia's sister, had told Sherlock Holmes. "A vague feeling of impending misfortune impressed me."

Then a scream tore July's sleep. He woke with a start. Had he been the only one to hear it—like the low, clear whistle that only the murdered sister had heard for several nights before her death? On the other side of the partition, Liberty slept on, dreaming of the skin of the night and imagining other universes. But there had been a scream—silent, but nonetheless a scream. And it still hung in the air.

10

A Man with a Lisp: Or Freak-Out Time at the Tower of London

"I REALLY DO FIND the silver sharks kind of scary," Zanny was saying. They were in a pet store. Madeline Starbuck had left that morning on a flight back to Washington, and Zanny had planned a day full of fun things to cheer the children up since they would not be seeing their mother for several weeks. The first stop of the day was the pet store on Wigmore Street that specialized in exotic fish.

"Yes, Madame, and they don't really get along all that well with spotted golds and the stripers the children seem to favor."

"Did you hear that, Charly and Molly?" Zanny asked the twins. They were mesmerized by the miniature predators slicing their way through the water in the tank.

"Guppies are always good," Liberty offered.

"Ah, but didn't you say you had a rather large pond in your garden room?" the man asked.

"Yes," replied Zanny. "I think it's about this wide and this deep." She showed him with her hands.

"Well, then these fish, the spotted golds and the stripers, would do splendidly."

Liberty loved the way the English used the word "splendid." It was such a truly glittering word and fit certain things so nicely—these bright gold fish, for example. "Yes," the man continued. "I should think these fish might grow to quite an impressive size given the dimensions of your pool."

Charly looked up from under her coonskin cap. "Like *Jaws?*" she said and grinned.

"Oh, dear, I should hope not!" the man said. "Now where did you two get those interesting hats? And what do you call them?"

"Davy Crockett caps. Our grandma gave them to us."

"Davy Crockett?"

"He was a guy," Molly said. "A frontier guy."

"He died at the Alamo," July added.

"Oh," said the fish man, then changed the subject. "So will it be the spotted golds and the stripers?"

It was the spotted golds and the stripers. Two of each. They took them back to the house in the mews, and on their way they checked in with the lady at the florist's. She had just set aside two beautiful pale pink water lilies for them, so she scooped them up, roots and all, and put them in a bag of water.

The water in the pool was just the right temperature, and they put the fish and the lilies in as soon as they got home. There were great arguments about what to name the fish, but names were finally settled on. They were Charly's and Molly's choices—Davy and Madeline, and Barbie and Ken.

"I think it's weird naming a fish after Mom," Liberty said. But she wasn't prepared to argue about it. They were eager to get on to the next stop of the day: The Tower of London.

" 'Many places in Britain seem to attract ghosts of all sizes and shapes, but the greatest number of spooks undoubtedly reside in the Tower of London.' " Zanny was reading from a guidebook as she and the children stood on a rampart. The rampart stretched over a waterless moat now green with grass, and it led into the Tower of London. She continued reading: " 'There's no telling what you might find in the dark passageways and silent rooms of the Tower, but it's said that you may run into anyone or anything, from regiments of long-dead soldiers to Anne Boleyn herself.' "

The Tower was not, to the children's surprise, a single simple tower, but a fortress. Zanny had given them a list, illustrated with small drawings of heads that she had traced, of all the famous people who had been held prisoner and had been beheaded in the Tower of London. A special tour had been arranged for them through the American embassy, and not two minutes after they had given their names at the gate, a man approached them.

He was wearing a broad-brimmed black hat with a deep crown and red decorations. His scarlet jacket was full of embroidery and had puff-ball shoulders. The britches he wore stopped at the knees and were met by hose, or tights. Clanking with swords and medallions, he cut a striking figure as a yeoman warder, or a beefeater, as the guards of the Tower were more popularly known.

"The Starbuck party!" he exclaimed heartily. Never was there a man who could talk more cheerfully and crack more jokes about the beheadings and the grim doings that had occurred in a previous age at the Tower of London. Yeoman Jack began the tour by leading them up to a display of weaponry and torture equipment in one of the Tower's galleries. They then proceeded to the Tower Green. Cheerfully he ticked off the names of the most famous victims to lose their heads there on Tower Green. Of these famous ones, only Anne Boleyn was executed with a sword. The rest had been killed with an ax. The twins scrunched up their shoulders as they imagined these beheadings.

Gruesome thoughts crackled between them as they wondered about having their heads chopped off.

Which would feel better, a sword or an ax?

An ax would be heavier.

Maybe it would make it quicker.

How 'bout a butter knife? Molly telewondered.

Nearby, another beefeater was giving a similar account to a large group of tourists. Both beefeaters had now reached the part of the story where they were telling about the beheading of Mary, Queen of Scots. "And," said Jack, "the Scottish queen went composed and well dressed to her death. She wore her lovely auburn hair piled high in the style of the day. But would you believe it? After the ax fell, the head of the queen of Scots rolled, and the executioner went to pick it up"—He paused dramatically and held his hand in the air as if holding an imaginary head. Then he continued, "Well, my goodness! The hair came off in his hands. For the queen was nearly bald except for a few strands of dull gray hair on her rather small head." The children and Zanny all gasped.

The other beefeater was just about at the same point in the story. He had a slight lisp, and to July and Liberty the voice had a vaguely familiar quality. "And ven," the other beefeater continued, "the executioner vent to pick up the 'ead"—a chill ran through both the twins—"Surprise, it vas a vig!"

Wiper viper

Vig wig

W's and *v*'s seemed to crash silently in the air. Their blood ran cold.

The air filled with static.

J. B.! J%##@B

Lib&&%##^@

Liberty was losing him again. She knew it!

She had been concentrating so hard on July that she had not noticed that the lisping beefeater was approaching Charly and Molly. Liberty stood transfixed.

She could hear tiny cracklings. The little twins' communication was breaking up, too! It was dwindling off into the dimmest flickerings. All she could think of was dying fireflies on a summer night, just like the ones Molly and Charly always kept in their jars too long. Except now it was their turn to flicker out. . . .

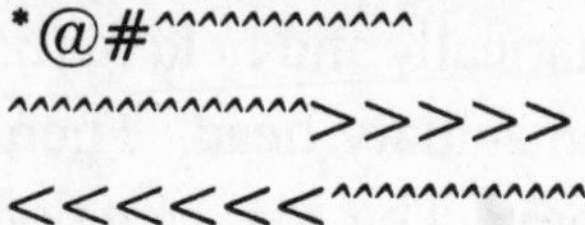

As if in slow motion, the beefeater plucked Charly's and Molly's coonskin caps off their heads and said, "And the queen of Scots's hair was red as these two little darlings'!" The words curdled in the air. Everything was static. Liberty felt herself helplessly being drawn to the edge of that dreadful abyss again. She couldn't bear that feeling of oncoming separateness; she could not cross over. She gasped weakly and fainted.

Yeoman Jack cleared the area quickly. "Stand back, please. Kindly stand back! Give the girl a little room. Move your group along, sir," he said to the other beefeater. The man and his group seemed to vanish in a flash. "Who the devil is that bloke?" Yeoman Jack muttered to himself.

The other children and Zanny were all on their knees, clustered around Liberty.

"Is she dead?" wailed Molly.

"Of course I'm not dead." Liberty's eyes flew open. "Just a little . . ." She paused. "A little . . ." But she could not find the word. Jack helped her to her feet.

"I'm not sure what happened." She blinked at Molly and Charly. Their coonskin caps were planted firmly on their heads. They looked fine. She looked around for the other beefeater. He was nowhere in sight. She looked at July.

I felt it this time, Liberty. It was terrible.

There was the static, and then there was nothing?

Worse than nothing. They weren't just invading the channels; it was me! I felt locked. I had to fight it so hard. You don't know how hard. I felt myself slipping away, and I felt your fear. I felt you standing there at the abyss and me not being able to help you.

July did not look good, but Liberty doubted if she looked much better. His skin was deathly pale, his freckles stood out like a terrible rash, and his clear gray eyes were certainly not vacant this time, but full of a fear she could recognize.

But you must have done something, J. B., because look, the channels are clear now.

Yeah, but look at you. You fainted.

You don't look so hot yourself.

Zanny actually looked worse than any of them despite the fact that she kept her voice even in a smooth flow of reassuring words.

"It's all right, kids. I'm sure it's just a little tummy upset."

Play it as a tummy upset, Liberty.

I guess you're right, but I still think she might be suspicious. I mean, that guy was weird. She noticed it, too, I'm sure. "Yeah, this English food, Zanny, it's starting to get to me. Do we really have to include it in the English curriculum?"

"You mean you'd enjoy a minor lapse?"

"Yeah, right into a McDonald's. I think a Coke and some fries would set me up just fine."

"Okay, but are you sure you're all right?"

"I'm all right—just like you said, a tummy upset."

But the words sounded hollow. Jack insisted they come with him to the yeomen's quarters so Liberty could have "a bit of a sit and a cup of tea."

Everyone was very kind and concerned. They brought the children Coca-Colas and biscuits, as the English called cookies, and brought tea for Zanny. The twins felt rather small and insignificant in a room filled with large men decked out in scarlet, each one clanking with metal and carrying at least a pound of gold embroidery.

"I say," Jack said to one of the beefeaters. "Do we have a new man on today? Saw one I didn't recognize."

"New man?" said the other. "Let me think. Ah yes, I believe there is a new bloke on this morning. He's filled in a couple of times this month when someone's out sick. Can't say I care for him all that much. He does the bit all right, but he has an odd twist to his speech. I think he comes over from Lambeth Road area, you know, St. Thomas's Hospital."

It can't be! July tele-exclaimed.

But then Liberty said it. "St. Thomas's Hospital?"

"Yes," said the man. "Do you know it?"

"Not really," she said and took another swallow of her Coke.

11

Stretch Limo Birthday Blast

What if the chauffeur is the man from Pinchin Lane, the beefeater?

For one split second the most dreadful thought passed through both July's and Liberty's heads. The children were standing on the corner of Wimpole and Devonshire awaiting the birthday limo. For indeed the car was too stretched to make the turn into the mews. They were beside themselves with excitement.

"I see it!" cried Molly.

"It's coming!" Charly jumped up and down, shouting.

That was when the terrible thought flashed through the older twins' heads. The terrible *What if.*

The days had slipped by rather quickly, and the memory of the incident at the Tower of London seemed to recede as their excitement about July and Liberty's upcoming birthday grew. But now the dreadful thought seemed to lash the air around them as the long silver limo turned right from New Cavendish Street onto

Wimpole. Liberty and July nearly collapsed with relief when a young woman with glasses and short-cropped brown hair jumped out. The two flag holders on either side of the hood of the limo proudly flew red and blue balloons.

"July Burton Starbuck," she said, "also known as J. B. and Jelly Bean, and Liberty Bell Starbuck, happy birthdays! I am your chauffeur, Kate." She held out her hand and shook hands first with July. "I understand you beat your sister into this world by four minutes." She then turned to Liberty and shook her hand, too. "Step this way." Kate opened one of the rear curbside doors and July stepped in, followed by his sister.

"Oh wow!" Liberty exclaimed. The interior of the limo had been decorated with streamers and balloons, and there was a Happy Birthday sign, too.

"Cool."

"Cool."

"Cool." The word was uttered at least twenty times in the first minute and a half.

"Where's the makeup counter?" Charly and Molly immediately wanted to know. They had decided to bring the makeup kits Aunt Honey had given them for Christmas. The idea of putting on lipstick and perfume while in a moving car was an exciting one. That was all they seemed to think about.

Liberty and July did not have makeup on their minds. They had been more concerned with planning the picnic. Now, with Zanny's help, they stashed the food in two built-in refrigerators. There were sandwiches and cold drinks, plenty of junk-food snacks, and, of course, two birthday cakes. That was rule number one of twindom: twins should never have to share a birthday cake. Madeline had read about this early on, when she had first become the mother of twins, in a magazine called the *Twinsey Report*. If she hadn't read it, she might have remembered from her own childhood, and failing that, the twins would have told her immediately.

There wasn't room in the limo's freezer for ice cream, so they decided to stop and get it if they really needed it. After all, it was Jelly Bean and Liberty's birthday, and as the Starbuck family birthday saying went, Birthday is Boss Day. They had never bothered to translate this family motto into Latin. The limo trip would wind up at the ambassador's residence for a Fourth of July party complete with fireworks.

"Where to?" Kate asked from the front of the car. Her voice came over an intercom.

Their first stop was the British Museum to take in a few mummies and the famous Elgin Marbles that Zanny had told them the English had stolen from the Parthenon of ancient Greece. The Greeks had never forgiven the English for this theft.

After the museum and back in the limo the children broke out an early-morning snack of nachos and salsa on their way to Greenwich, the very spot, not far from the city of London, from which all time is measured and where standard time is set. "You'd think that the queen would be embarrassed about this," Liberty said, munching on a nacho.

"Embarrassed about what?" asked Zanny.

"Her people—ripping off the Greeks. I mean she's so proper and everything with her crown, and she's always wearing those white gloves in every single picture of her."

"Yeah," said July. "You don't think of her as harboring criminals."

"Well," interjected Kate from the front seat, "you know she's really just a figurehead. I mean, nice lady, but not much real power, and it happened long before her reign."

"What's a figurehead?" asked Molly.

"Yeah, and what's harboring?" asked Charly. It took the rest of the car trip to Greenwich to explain figurehead and harboring criminals to Charly and Molly.

From Greenwich they went on to four ancient castles, including one with a maze. A soft rain began to fall just when they pulled up to a meadow where they thought they would have their picnic. Instead they flicked on the television. They watched five minutes of "Gilligan's Island," and then it was "The Brady Bunch." Somehow the Brady Bunch looked really stupid singing away with their little freckled cheerful faces as the credits rolled by. The program was still on when they finished their sandwiches, and Kate started the limo. "This will clear off soon. I guarantee it," she said. "It will be fine by the time you're ready to eat your birthday cakes. Keep a sharp lookout for the right place."

"Okay," Liberty and July replied. They settled back in the comfortably upholstered seats and watched the rest of "The Brady Bunch."

How would we look if there was a television program called "The Starbuck Bunch"? Liberty wondered.

People would just think their TVs were broken, and they were getting double images, July tele-answered.

Charly and Molly had folded out the hideaway vanity. There were little compartments that slid open with combs and tissues and fancy lotions. They flipped up a double-sided mirror and chose the magnified side. Taking out their makeup kits, the twins began to put on lipstick and blushing powder. Their huge, twin images crowded into the frame.

"Move over, Molly," Charly said. "I can't fit my eye in. I want to put on some of this eye shadow." She was holding a little pot of chartreuse powder and was trying to dab some on her eyelid. She missed, leaving a yellow-green smudge by her ear instead.

"Girls, don't do eye makeup while we're moving. I'm afraid you'll poke out your eyes," Zanny said.

"Oh, Zanny!" sighed Charly.

"I know," said Zanny. "I'm incredibly boring and no fun at all. But please just wait with the eye makeup until we're stopped."

"How 'bout press-on nails?" Molly asked.

They all, except for Molly and Charly, groaned at

the mention of this. Press-on fingernails had been a subject of much controversy since before they had even left for England. Everyone, except for Molly and Charly, hated the notion of these little tykes going around with fake fingernails that looked like miniature daggers. The press-on nails had been at the top of their Christmas lists and birthday lists since they were four years old. And Aunt Honey had always obliged them. Both July and Liberty had tried their best to humiliate the little twins by saying that Mary and Laura Ingalls in *Little House on the Prairie* would have never wanted or worn press-on nails. But the twins did an end run around that argument. "They weren't invented then, and if they had been, and Mary and Laura had known about them, they would have wanted them!" It was difficult to argue.

"Okay," sighed Zanny. "You can put them on, but remember to take them off before we go to the party this evening at the ambassador's house."

What does the ambassador know about Mary and Laura, anyhow? Molly teleflashed.

Yeah, I bet Mr. and Mrs. Ambassador would like press-on *^^^*^^^

Uh oh ^**^*^^^*^^

Charly again tried to flash the words "press-on nails," but the strange static was happening again—the tiny cracklings like the ones that had filled the air just before Liberty had fainted at the Tower. The little twins were not disturbed by the static. They thought of it as a temporary interruption rather than an invasion of their telepathic channels. And since they knew nothing of the events in Pinchin Lane, they gave it no thought. Instead they quickly became absorbed in the business of putting on their nails.

Neither July nor Liberty seemed aware of any problem. They were looking out the window of the limo at the passing countryside.

The sun had just started to break through when the road dropped down into a little gully. There was a small stone bridge ahead, and the dark water of the river ran smooth as a black satin ribbon around a deep bend. The woods had trees that looked older than time, and in the very same instant July and Liberty both blurted out, "That's the place!"

"The cake place, you mean?" Kate's voice came through the intercom.

"Yes!" both Liberty and July shouted.

"Looks perfect to me," said Kate. She slowed down immediately.

"Why, kids, it's more than perfect," Zanny said, looking at her guidebook.

"What do you mean?" July and Liberty asked.

"We're in Sussex, right?"

"Right," said Kate.

"And hadn't you kids mentioned that Conan Doyle's home in his later years was here?"

"Yes," said July.

"Look ahead." Zanny nodded toward the front of

the limo. On the other side of the road, where the land opened up beyond the woods, five gables scratched at the now-blue sky.

"It's Windlesham!" July exclaimed.

"Yes, I do believe you're right," Kate said, looking at a map. "And I think that Conan Doyle was buried here."

Are you scared, Liberty?

No, don't be stupid.

But do you feel the echoes?

Yes, but it's kind of weird. They aren't as loud as they are back in the house.

I know. I was thinking the same thing. You know what these woods are called? July asked.

No. What? Liberty was almost afraid to know.

Slaughter Glen.

J. B., you're trying to scare me.

No, really.

Do you hear a funny crackling sound, not really like static?

I'm receiving you fine.

It must be the little twins. They might be breaking up a little.

Oh no!

Don't worry.

But July could sense that Liberty was still worried about the little twins. Was there perhaps more to the crackling and breaking up in their telepathy than met the eye? Funny things, scary things had happened to twins before in Holmes stories. A chill went down his spine as he remembered Bartholomew Sholto's death by poison dart. And wasn't there another set of twins in another story? Next to him Liberty fidgeted and bit nervously on her index finger. July stopped his thoughts before his sister could tune in.

You know how they get when it's not their birthday. Probably just the strain of not being the center of attention for one day a year. Anyhow, as I was saying, I read something in a book about how Doyle's study looked right out on this clump of trees, and he would tell people about the times long before when smugglers and highwaymen and gypsies used to hide out in these woods.

And steal birthday cakes, no doubt, and prey upon innocent kids. No, I'm not scared. This is a perfect place for our party.

So it was decided, and both the birthday cakes, Liberty's decorated with stars and stripes and July's with exploding firecrackers, were brought out. They spread the tablecloth and put out paper plates. Kate brought matches from the car, and she lit one set of candles while Zanny lit the others. The candles held steady in the light wind as Zanny, Kate, Charly, and Molly sang "Happy Birthday." Sunlight streamed through the gnarled branches of the old trees, and just as they were singing the very end of the last verse, Liberty thought she saw Molly's eyes focus on something beyond them, just off in the trees. But she was concentrating on gathering her breath to blow out the candles and didn't turn to look.

"Happy birthday, July and Liberty!" July and Liberty were crouched on their knees about to blow out the candles when a sudden wind blew up.

The wind will help you blow out your candles, July, Liberty teleflashed.

Do I seem that old? July began. But then something happened.

A terrible laugh filled the very center of the wind, and Liberty saw Charly's and then Molly's faces freeze into masks of terror. And the wind, Liberty thought as she exhaled mightily, did not seem to be helping at all. One candle's flame was still wavering on her cake and so was one on July's. Then she heard Zanny scream.

It all happened so fast it was hard to know the precise order. But Zanny seemed to grab one cake and both small twins at the same time. Kate grabbed the other cake. Out of the depths of Slaughter Glen, a figure of a man had appeared, and he was holding a stick. On the stick was a snake, a live speckled snake.

"Just a vee wiper!" The snake writhed on the end of the stick, its diamond-shaped head swaying, the forked tongue striking out, the neck puffed in fury.

How she ever got all the children and the cakes into the car Zanny would never know. She sank back against the upholstered seat.

"I can't believe it!" Kate exclaimed through the intercom. "I mean, I don't scare easily, but that bloke was terrible and up to no good." They were roaring along the road. July and Liberty still peered in stunned disbelief out the rear window.

It can't be true.

Are you sure?

Count the candles, July. You saw it as well as I did. You saw him standing there.

They didn't want to say it out loud, and they didn't even want to think it or teleflash it. And although you can stop words spoken out loud, both twins knew it was almost impossible to banish telepathic images. Now one was crackling in their brains. Only they had seen it. The man—and it was the same man who had been a beefeater at the Tower, with the same voice as the man on Pinchin Lane—had walked over to the very spot where they had been blowing out the candles. As the car drove off, the twins had watched him. Slowly he had bent over. Two candles were still burning on the ground, the same two candles July and Liberty had failed to blow out when the wind had come up. The man had picked them up, held them, and simply stared at the children with a trace of the most awful grin on his face. That was their last view of him from the limo as Kate sped away.

Slowly, July turned around in his seat and sank back. The limo was a mess, crumbs and frosting all over. And candles, yes, there were candles. He began to count them slowly. Liberty was right. There were twenty-four candles—one for each of their twelve years. Yet two candles were missing: the two to grow on.

12

Firecrackers and Thunderheads: An Electrical Storm to Remember

JULY AND LIBERTY couldn't get that awful scene out of their heads: the two small flames of those birthday candles flickered with a terrible brilliance. And the fireworks now at the ambassador's house were doing little to erase the image. They were being pursued, that was for sure, but why and for what and by whom? What had they done to deserve this?

Apparently it didn't bother Zanny. And this worried both July and Liberty. She seemed to doubt what she had just seen.

"Zanny," Liberty blurted out, "there was a man standing there in broad daylight holding a snake on a stick."

"He could have just been a naturalist, a snake collector out on an afternoon stroll."

Unbelievable! July flashed. *Absolutely unbelievable.*

I think she was bewitched. She was as scared as we

were, and now she's trying to pass this guy off as a naturalist, some bird-watcher type!

"You have to realize, children . . ."

*Oh, crimin**ey! Whenever she calls us children you know she's heading off in the wrong direction. Trying to be* Ms. *Super Adult*, Liberty flashed to July.

I know. Can you believe it? She's ready to blow this whole thing off. In another ten seconds she's going to be getting into psychology and all that stuff, July flashed back.

It took Zanny about eight seconds to get to the psychology part. "You have to realize we have been in a heightened state of anxiety since we've come to a foreign country. It makes us more psychologically susceptible, more inclined to twist things in our minds. Well, not twist things, but we get a little paranoid and might think we're seeing one thing while it might be entirely different."

"Wait a minute. Hold it right there," Liberty said. "Do you agree that you saw a man coming out of the woods holding a snake?"

"Well, yes, but it was a delusion on your part that he was actually threatening you in any way."

Delusion, she calls it! July flashed.

Delusion, my foot.

Delusion, my brain—see, I told you it would take her about ten seconds to get to the psychology part. I think it was less.

Zanny was turning into your standard grown-up. This was what always happened to grown-ups, even the best ones like Zanny who most of the time didn't act like total grown-ups. They come home, take a shower like Zanny had, get relaxed, and then decide the kids are nuts and have to be taught a lesson or two.

"It wasn't a delusion," Liberty said. "And I saw the look on your face, Zanny. You were scared, too."

"Okay, I admit I was frightened. The guy was definitely weird. Maybe he wasn't a naturalist. I think he was just . . ." Zanny hesitated. "You know, your run-of-the-mill pervert who jumps out of the woods and scares people. You know, like those people who enjoy making dirty phone calls."

Zanny could tell the twins were not buying this. Looking back at it now, it seemed very childish to think she had become so frightened and almost panicked the moment the strange man stepped out of the woods. She had to realize the Starbuck children were not ordinary in the least. Highly imaginative, very articulate. It was easy to get drawn into their world, to cross over some imaginary line between the adult world of logic and order into their fanciful world.

So according to Zanny we've just got a run-of-the-mill pervert here, July flashed.

Yeah, like those guys who make dirty phone calls, and it might not be just one. It could be three different perverts, Liberty answered.

Jeez, how lucky can you get? July sighed. The sigh was like a little glimmer in the air between them.

Well, Liberty flashed back, *when you're two sets of*

twins I guess you call it not luck exactly, but double trouble squared.

Liberty recalled that conversation now as fireworks exploded above her on the ambassador's lawn. She found it disheartening. She had thought that there might have been a possibility of letting Zanny in on all of this. Apparently that was not to be. It was now up to July and herself. That was a little bit scary.

She focused on Charly and Molly, who were sitting on the grass in front of her. Charly had just licked her runny nose with her tongue, a talent both little twins shared. They could stick their tongues straight up and wipe the space between their upper lips and the bottom of their noses. Their tongues were just like little windshield wipers. It was exceedingly gross. Why then did the little twins seem so suddenly precious to her? How could they be so dear and so gross at the same time—these annoying little snot-nosed twerps. They licked their upper lips again. Liberty hoped the ambassador's wife wasn't watching them. Mrs. Whitmore was very proper.

They look like doggies!

Just like Pookie. The lady looks like Pookie.

The little twins were silently discussing the ambassador's family, specifically his wife. Liberty knew what they were saying in a general way, not word for word. Sometimes she could only get glimmerings. And right now the glimmerings seemed to match up with Liberty's own thinking. Ambassador Whitmore and his wife and two daughters all looked like dogs. Mrs. Whitmore—Lulu—looked exactly like Pookie, Aunt Honey's Pekingese. She had thick, silky dark blond hair that bushed out around her head. Her face was smushed up toward her forehead—the lip curled toward the nose, the nose pointed straight up, just like a Pekingese. She would have had no trouble licking a runny nose with her tongue if she had been that gross. But she wasn't.

Ambassador Whitmore was large with coal black hair and heavy black eyebrows. His cheeks seemed to collapse into puddles of flesh around his mouth, and if the ambassador wasn't a human version of a black Lab, then Liberty didn't know who was. The two teenage daughters, Isabelle and Fifi, were another breed entirely. They were punk versions of Chihuahuas. Small and painfully skinny, they both wore their hair extremely short, and like Chihuahuas they had slightly pointy ears and bulgy eyes. They had lots of eye makeup on and wore teeny tiny miniskirts with stars-and-stripes stockings. They were very nice to the children, though, and they gave them little colored stars to stick on their faces. Liberty just hoped Molly and Charly wouldn't say anything about how much the Whitmores looked like dogs. And of course she hoped they wouldn't lick their snotty noses in front of Ambassador and Mrs. Whitmore.

Liberty heard Mrs. Whitmore apologizing for how Fifi and Isabelle were dressed, which didn't make her think much of Mrs. Whitmore as a mother. Ambassador and Mrs. Whitmore slobbered a lot over the little twins, and nobody seemed to notice they had neglected to take off their press-on nails.

"Remarkable! Remarkable!" Ambassador Whitmore kept saying. "And to think of two sets in one family. Handsome lot you've got there, Put! I'll be! Gracious sakes, must keep your wife busy. Oh that's right, she's tending the store. Har dee har, har har. Women's lib. You know about Madeline Starbuck, Lulu, don't you? Real dynamo, that woman!" Ambassador Whitmore was full of meaningless, hearty phrases.

"Yes, I've heard of her. I was telling Lady Aberdeen about her just the other day. You know Lady Aberdeen, Mr. Starbuck? She's a lady-in-waiting to the queen, and . . ." Lulu Whitmore was dropping royal names right and left. Liberty could see that Fifi and Isabelle found their mother as embarrassing as their mother found their clothing.

"Lady Lulu's at it again!" she heard Isabelle whisper to Fifi.

"Bet she wishes she had more than these second-string royals here tonight," Fifi said.

Liberty could not contain her curiosity. "Is the royal family here tonight?"

"Hardly!" said Fifi, sticking a star back on her cheek. "These are just sub-royals," she said, looking around. "A few titles but none with really good court connections. No one from Kensington Palace."

A rumble of thunder was followed by a roll of groans.

"Let's hope the rest of these fireworks beat the rain," the ambassador's voice boomed. "Else it's going to be Ping-Pong indoors!" Just at that moment Lulu called to him.

What a wit! Liberty flashed.

He's not paid to be a wit. He's paid to be cordial, that's all. Dad does most of the thinking for him and runs the embassy. The ambassador's very diplomatic. That's his job. You're too hard on him, Liberty.

The fireworks beat out the rain by twenty minutes, and by the time they arrived back at Number 3, Devonshire Mews, it was pouring buckets.

13

The Crack in the Eaves

THE HOUSE IN THE MEWS felt cozy and welcoming when they returned. The corners were steeped in shadows, which, despite the few lights Put turned on, seemed thicker than ever.

Both July and Liberty had a funny feeling they were at some kind of a turning point, and not simply because they had turned twelve that day. No, something more was beginning to happen within the house. They climbed the steps to their attic bedroom.

The rain came down harder. July turned on the little radio he had received for his birthday. As they got ready for bed, they heard the BBC weatherman read the maritime report. With his clipped speech and even tone he was like the calm eye at the center of the storm. "There are warnings of gales in the Solent, Shannon, Fastnet, Irish Sea, the Hebrides, Bay of Biscay, Portland, Plymouth, Strait of Dover. Good sailing, chaps."

"My goodness, isn't he cheerful. The nerve!" Put

had come up to the attic to wish his children happy birthday and to kiss them good night. "There he sits in his cozy little studio warning of gales in every quadrant the BBC covers, and he wishes the sailors good sailing. It's a messy night," Put said, looking out the dormer windows as ragged, oily-looking clouds tore across the moon-streaked night. The sky looked like ashes.

Again Put wished them happy birthday, hugged them, and told them to get to sleep. Liberty did this promptly. But as exhausted as he was, July couldn't fall asleep. Supposing, he thought, that the man from Slaughter Glen found them. He heard Liberty turn over in bed. This thought must have disturbed her.

July's mind ran on. Suppose that the light of the two birthday candles led the man right to this place, to the attic. A chill ran down his spine. Liberty moaned a little. There would be no sleeping tonight. He suddenly felt hungry. He climbed out of bed and walked over to the desk he shared with Liberty. The speckled band of M&M's dividing the territory had been eaten up the week before. Now there was a line of jelly beans along the tape. He picked one up and ate it. After all the junk food he had eaten today, his mother would call this an outrageous assault on his gut. Oh well, his nickname was Jelly Bean, he thought, as he popped in the pink, minty-tasting candy.

Just as he turned to go to bed, J. B. froze. Something was wrong. He peered more closely at the speckled band. They had just filled it in the evening before, but several jelly beans were missing. They couldn't have eaten that many, especially when they had been gone all day. This was J. B.'s first since they had filled them in last night. When they had gotten up this morning, the line was complete. He remembered no gaps, and he hadn't noticed Liberty eating any before she went to bed. Charly and Molly hardly ever came up to the attic. They had fallen asleep coming home in the car from the ambassador's residence. Put and Zanny had carried them in. So it wasn't them. Could it be a mouse?

July looked down at the tape. In the gaps where jelly beans had been he could see dim little bean-shaped blotches, like colored shadows. They were very pale, some pink, some orange, some green—the colors of jelly beans. It was very odd. Had they dissolved into thin air, leaving only a ghostly trace behind? He rubbed his forehead. Was he seeing things?

July felt restless. He was tired, and yet he knew he could not sleep. He put on his bathrobe and walked over to the window. The rain thrummed against the panes so hard that the drops were squashed flat into a black glaze of water. The night and the rain made a mirror of the glass, and July looked at his face in it. His face appeared slightly blurred like a watercolor that was still wet. He didn't look old, and he didn't look young. He didn't look very real, either, he thought.

Then the rhythm of the rain changed. The wind changed, too. It lessened. Everything seemed to ease and slow up. The water made runnels down the pane, and he watched the image of his face break into pieces like those of a jigsaw puzzle.

There was a puzzle about this house in the mews, but it wasn't him. He turned to go to bed. But in that sliver of an instant, out of the corner of his eye, he caught a small flickering in one of the windowpanes. A twin flickering, actually, as from two little flames.

His blood froze, and his feet simply would not move. He was too afraid to turn around and face the window but also too curious to run to bed. Finally, very slowly, he raised the polished surface of his digital watch to catch the reflection. On the scratched and distorted watch face he caught the two flickering licks of flame, the reflection of two birthday candles! He cried out, wheeled around, but the windowpane was perfectly black with beating rain.

He stared in disbelief. He knew he had seen the twin images of those flickering birthday candles, but now they were gone. Liberty had not even awakened when he screamed. He made his way shakily to bed and climbed in, drawing the comforter right up to his ears. He watched shadows gather around him. He had never felt so alone in his life.

July did not know how long he had been asleep, but something woke him. He was not sure whether it was the thunder or the lightning, but the night had turned wild. A full gale tore at the house, and the air outside had an eerie luminescence as lightning fractured the sky. The profiles of rooftops and chimney pots were limned in the harsh light of the storm's fierce electrical display. The chimney behind Liberty's bed gulped great downward drafts of air and seemed to alternately moan and hiccup and gasp. Liberty could sleep through anything, July thought. And then the most ferocious bolt of all exploded directly overhead.

A flash filled the room with a sickly unnatural light. Within that flash, July caught sight of an almost imperceptible crack in the corner of the attic across from his bed. It was there, on the windowless side of the room, where the ceiling of the attic dropped down beneath the eaves of the house. What was it? It seemed too regular to be the kind of random crack one might find in an old ceiling of an old house. Ventilators and bell ropes! The words from the Sherlock Holmes story came back. The bell rope was there "as a bridge for something passing through the hole, and coming to the bed," a bridge for a swamp adder, or that snake on the stick from that afternoon!

July was rigid with fear. He buried his head under the covers. He heard Liberty moan softly in her sleep and turn over. He was too scared to call to her, but he knew that somewhere deep within her dreams she was feeling his fear, his anxiety. Oh, for this night to be over! July thought of Dr. Watson's description of the sound he and Sherlock had heard: "a very gentle, soothing sound, like that of a small jet of steam escaping continually from a kettle." That was how he had described the noise the snake had made as it descended the bell rope to strike its victim. But as frightened as J. B. was, it became difficult to hold his eyes open. His eyelids fluttered and sagged. This day, this night, had been too much. His eyes felt so heavy. He tried to keep them open. He thought of the awnings shopkeepers unrolled every morning on Marylebone High Street. It was as if some shopkeeper, a shopkeeper of sleep, was unrolling his eyelids, letting them down. What a silly thought. He yawned. His eyes opened slightly again and then drooped. Did he hear a soft whistling, a low clear whistle in the night? Oh gee, hadn't the horrible man called back the swamp adder by whistling? No, no, that was just the wind in the chimney. Was he really too tired now even to be frightened? The shopkeeper won.

14

"There Is a Presence Here"

"THERE'S THE SCARLET THREAD of murder running through the colourless skein of life, and our duty is to unravel it, and isolate it, and expose every inch of it." The words that now ran through July's mind were from the Sherlock Holmes story *A Study in Scarlet*. But of course July was not looking at a scarlet thread but a very faded speckled band, and he was not feeling smart.

It was the following evening. That morning, July had told Liberty about his sleepless night, starting with the missing jelly beans, moving on to the flickering image of the lost birthday candles. For some reason, he had not told her about the crack in the ceiling. He supposed he had held back because he related the crack to the bell rope and the snake. He knew how fearful his sister was of snakes. He didn't want to scare her unnecessarily. He also knew that Liberty was aware that he was holding back. She could sense these things, but today she did not choose to push it.

"Whoever has been eating these does not like the

yellow ones," July said, scratching his head. He looked over at Liberty. She was totally absorbed in her reading—research, she said, but for the life of him he couldn't figure out how reading a book on the development and personalities of twins would help her with this. He turned off the desk light and was about to get up and go to bed when he noticed a dim glow that seemed to radiate from the tape.

"Good grief!" July exclaimed. "Liberty, come over here."

"What is it?" She looked up from her bed.

"The jelly-bean spots—they're glowing in the dark!"

Liberty leaped off her bed and came over.

"Incredible!" She stared down at the softly glowing pools of color.

"I wonder what they're doing to our guts if they do this to the tape?"

Yuck, they both thought as they imagined a speckled band of Day-Glo jelly beans coiled in their intestines. They were both locked in silence, but the air crackled with their telepathic communications.

This is very curious, Liberty mused.

It's like a kind of afterimage, July flashed.

Afterimage?

You remember in science when we were studying the human eye? After the image is formed on the retina, it's only there for a fraction of a second before it fades to form the next image. Remember the experiments we did when we looked at a switched-on light bulb and then closed our eyes and could still see it? That's the afterimage. Maybe that would explain the reflections of the birthday candles I saw last night in the window, or rather on my watch face.

Yeah, I guess so. It's how they do animated cartoons in the movies.

Right. You think it's all one smooth moving picture, but it's twenty-four different ones in one second. The afterimages in your brain are what smooth it all out. They call it persistence of vision.

What do these jelly-bean spots have to do with all that? Liberty telewondered.

I don't know.

"We have got to start deducting and detecting just like Holmes would," Liberty continued, speaking out loud.

She was right. Up until now they had just been letting the shadows gather around them, confounding and confusing them. It was time to start thinking.

"You're right, Liberty," J. B. said. "Crime is common. Logic is rare. Therefore, it is upon logic rather than crime that you should dwell."

Oh, bravo, bravo!

The words flashed through the air. Liberty's eyes opened wide.

"Not me!" July mouthed the words.

"The other voice," Liberty whispered. Suddenly, the air seemed to fill with the static of hundreds of different transmitters. It was as if there was an electrical storm in their heads. Then it subsided as suddenly as it had begun.

Liberty shut her eyes tight for a moment and shook her head vigorously, trying to clear out the last remnants of static. "Let's get back to logic, okay? What's with that crack you refuse to talk about?"

So she had guessed it despite his efforts to keep the crack a secret.

"You were keeping me awake with it in your dreams all night."

"You were not that awake, Liberty, believe me. You sleep like a log."

"Well, start there anyway."

July explained what he thought he had seen illuminated in the flash of lightning during the electrical storm. Ten minutes later, Liberty was standing on a stool, examining the ceiling beneath the eaves. Nothing seemed unusual. Where he thought he had seen the crack, there was a kind of painted-over seam. Then again, seams spread at regular intervals all over the attic room where Sheetrock, a wall covering used instead of plaster, had been installed. Yet when Liberty looked down at July, her face was quite pale.

"There is a presence here," she whispered. "I feel it. I'm not hearing it or anything. It's not just the voice. I feel it breathing almost. We are very near to it."

"Get down," J. B. said. "Let me get up there."

Liberty climbed down from the stool, and July went

up. She was right. Something was there. The air seemed to almost tingle, and yet to the eye it appeared no different from any other wall or ceiling surface in the room.

Whether it was intuition or just a stab in the dark, neither one would ever know. Suddenly Liberty wanted to consult her twins research literature again. Meanwhile J. B. got out his magnifying glass and began to examine the area beneath the eaves. At this time of the night, the light was dim. His flashlight was out of batteries, and he could only drag a floor lamp so far. So instead he settled on examining the colored spots left from the vanished jelly beans.

July tried to apply some simple deduction to the prints. Stains had been left by the jelly beans, and furthermore they glowed in the dark. He tried to induct, to make a comparison of these facts to something similar, to go from the particular to the general, to the broader, bigger picture. But this was not July's strength in terms of reasoning and logic. Liberty was much better at perceiving the larger picture. Yet if he could do the deducting, figuring out the smaller bits, and Liberty could do the inducting, figuring out the larger parts, eventually their thoughts might come together like pieces of a patchwork quilt.

July kept thinking about the comparison of the stains to the afterimage left on the retina. The visual impression lingered after the object, the visual stimulus, was gone. He thought of the way animated film worked. He thought and he thought and he thought.

In what way were these stains like an afterimage—after what? He couldn't think another thought. It was Liberty's turn now.

She knew he had been thinking about all the afterimage stuff, and she too was thinking about it. She stayed up all that night reading. The notion of an afterimage had reminded her of something she had come across in the twins research for her school report.

When July woke up the next morning, Liberty was sitting up in bed looking alert. A pile of books and papers surrounded her.

"Finally!" she said. "Gads, talk about *me* sleeping like a log."

"Have you been up all night?" he asked, rubbing his eyes.

"No, I took a couple of catnaps, the last one just before dawn." She fixed him with a hard, serious look. "Now listen to this," she said.

"What? Have you come up with something?"

"Well, sort of. It's not exactly new, but it was something I was just led to. I'm not sure why, but I think it connects somehow with that afterimage stuff."

It's that disgusting thing, isn't it? That thing you read me before when you were doing your report?

It's not disgusting. It's science. Now don't go squishy on me.

But July was already feeling slightly nauseated. All this before breakfast. Well, maybe it was better that it was before breakfast on an empty stomach.

It's the van—

"—ishing twin theory." Liberty finished the word and the thought out loud. There was no sense pussyfooting around about this thing. She opened up her favorite book on twins, a big book illustrated with photographs and written by two women who were twins. "Listen to this," she said, and she began reading from the book.

" 'The bond between twins is often so strong that it remains even when one twin dies before or soon after birth. In one case, a doctor who had grown up as a single child had always felt a special affinity to twins—even to the point of dreaming he was a twin. When he mentioned these feelings to his mother'—" July started to scrunch up his face. He knew this part. Liberty had read this to him before. It made him shudder to think about how the man found out that he had a twin who had been born at the same time, except it had been a stillborn.

"Okay, okay," Liberty said quickly. "You know that part. I'll skip those details. But listen to this. This is definitely weird." She picked up a photocopy of a magazine article. " 'It is likely that many people may have had a twin before they were born, which could explain in biological terms the longing some singleton children have for an imagined long-lost twin.' " She stopped. "Now here's the biological basis."

"Is it yucky?" J. B. asked.

"No! No!" Liberty said and resumed reading the article. "It's just basically a miscarriage. Only one twin miscarries. The other doesn't and goes on to be born."

"That's all I want to know about that." He paused. "Now, why are you telling me all this? What does this vanishing twin business have to do with anything?"

Liberty's face suddenly went blank. Indeed she did not know why she had told him all this. But on the other hand, her face in its blankness was like a screen about to receive an image.

"Helen Stoner." She spoke softly. "In 'The Adventure of the Speckled Band.' She was a twin, wasn't she? Her sister who was murdered, bitten by the swamp adder, was her twin sister, wasn't she?"

"Yes," whispered July. He had felt it coming. All the time he had been thinking about the jelly-bean spots on the tape and the speckled band, he knew there had been something in the story he had avoided thinking about. On their birthday when Liberty had been so worried about Charly and Molly, hadn't he almost thought of the Stoner sisters then? But he'd pushed it from his mind. Helen and her murdered sister, Julia Stoner, had been twins.

Now simultaneously both July's and Liberty's attention was drawn back to the seam in the eaves. They could feel the tingling from where they sat. There was a presence, and the presence seemed at this moment to be filling the entire room. They could stand it no longer. Both children got up and bolted for the door.

Don't leave me! the voice cried out.

15

The Bow Street Runners

WHEN THE CHILDREN fled the room, it was not so much because they were frightened. It was rather that for a brief instant there was not enough room for all of them: July, Liberty, and whoever the third person, this presence, was. There did not seem to be enough air. July and Liberty headed in different directions out of the mews. Liberty went to a nearby park where Zanny had taken Charly and Molly to play. As soon as July had left the mews, he had begun to walk aimlessly down the street.

He had just turned the corner onto Devonshire when he heard a scolding voice curl out into the fresh morning air. It was coming from a house, a rather grand house on Devonshire Place that backed right up to the Starbucks' house in the mews. Indeed, their house had most likely been the stables for the grand house in a previous era.

"Now this is the last time I want to catch ye 'round here. Next time I call the bobbies. You and your tricks," the voice scolded. And then July saw a tiny figure, like a sooty smudge, streak down the block.

The figure stopped and looked directly at July, and although he did not beckon, July followed. He followed the figure for several blocks, through alleyways turning left and right, then left and left again. At one point the figure let him catch up a little. There was something eerie about the child, dirty, unkempt. His ill-fitting clothes did not look anything like the clothes children wore today. His pants stopped at the knees like knickers, and he wore a funny little torn double-breasted jacket. On his head he wore an odd cap with a ridiculously short bill that stuck out no more than an inch. His shoes were old-fashioned high-cut boots, so ragged that the toes of his left foot stuck out. He didn't look old, but you would never call him young despite his size. And though his face didn't look sad, it had certainly seen too much to look joyful.

July realized the strange little figure had led him to Baker Street, and he was going down the steps marking the entrance to the underground. July started to dig in his pocket for a 50p coin for his fare. The boy, however, winked and went right past the machine where people bought their tickets. Nonetheless, July went up to a machine where there was no line and quickly put in his money.

The ticket came out, and July was soon riding the long escalator down to the tracks. The boy was still ahead of him but in sight. July followed him through the passageways to the Jubilee Line, and they boarded the same car. But once July was in the car, the boy vanished. How could J. B. have lost him after all that?

There was no passing through the cars to search for him, but at Green Park, the second stop, he saw the boy exit onto the train platform. July was up and out of the car like a flash. He followed the boy to the Piccadilly Line track just as a train pulled in. This time he saw the boy get into another car. He definitely did not seem to want to ride in the same car as July. Okay, have it your way, July thought.

He was alert, though, and this time he stood near the door to see where the boy would get off. They passed through Piccadilly Circus and Leicester Square, but still the boy stayed on the train. Finally, at Covent Garden, July saw him get off. So July got off, too. He followed the boy up the stairs.

When they came up out of the underground, the boy was almost a block away. They crossed Bow Street and went half a block to an alley. And just under a sign, a black sign with gilt lettering, the boy seemed to vanish into thin air. The sign read The Bow Street Runners. Underneath were the words Specialists in Detective Literature. The entrance to the shop was just around the corner in the alleyway that passed between Bow Street and Drury Lane.

July went in. The light was dim and yellowish, as if filtered through old parchment paper. Everything was covered with a layer of dust, including the man behind the counter, who was speaking in a low, creaky voice to a couple. There was no sign of the boy. For a brief moment July hoped that the boy was the couple's son. It was an idiotic thought. The couple was American and dressed in contemporary clothes. The woman wore Reeboks, and the man had a little polo player on his striped shirt. There was no way the dirty smudgy kid with his torn jacket and high-cut boots belonged to these modern people.

"And so you see," the clerk with the creaky voice was saying, "the bobbies, our policemen, are a relatively new organization. They were only established about one hundred and fifty years ago. So in the time before the bobbies or even Scotland Yard, in the late eighteenth and early nineteenth centuries, a different kind of police organization existed in London. It was the Bow Street magistracy. And the Bow Street Runners were the constables attached to the court. This shop is named after them. They were the finest, the last word in detective work. They were brilliant in their performance. And this, of course, right here, was the center of it all. London at the time of the founding of the Bow Street Runners was a terrible, disease-ridden, squalid place filled with gin parlors, overrun by criminals. The runners began to solve some of the most notorious crimes that plagued the city—assaults, swindles, murders, kidnappings. The old police station was located just down the block. If you are a Sherlock Holmes fan, you might remember mention of Watson and Holmes coming to the old station in the story 'The Man with the Twisted Lip.' "

July's ears pricked up, and a shiver ran straight

down his spine. He thought the old boards of the shop would quake under him. The clerk wore a stiff, winged collar yellowed with age. It matched the sallowness of his skin, which was the color of old newspaper. He took off his wire-rimmed spectacles, and July swore a small cloud of dust fell as the man began rubbing them with a handkerchief. He looked toward July and squinted. "Are you interested in Sherlock Holmes, lad?"

"Yes. Yes, I guess I am."

"Well, you need not guess here," he said cheerfully. "We have the largest collection of Sherlockian materials in the world. Here's a new book right here, by a world expert on Sherlock and Sir Arthur Conan Doyle. This one covers his early years in London when he lived in Marylebone, up at the top of Wimpole Street. Devonshire Street, actually."

"He did?" July's eyes widened.

"He did indeed. I was just telling these good folks about the Bow Street Runners, for whom this shop is named. Now these were crack detectives, but it is thought that they employed small boys, little street ruffians, to do much of their legwork. You know a small boy, in dirty old London back then, could appear like another smudge on the scene and slip into places a full-grown man couldn't go without being noticed."

The image of the small boy, like a dirty streak on the shiny surface of a new morning, exploded in July's brain. What in the world was happening? First the man on Pinchin Lane, and now this.

The clerk continued, "And you see it is thought that perhaps Doyle used the small boys who helped the Bow Street Runners as his models or prototypes for the Baker Street Irregulars. Those are the youngsters Holmes referred to as the 'street Arabs,' the boys he employed to pick up vital information."

Of course that was it! That was why the boy had had an eerie familiarity to him and yet looked like something from another century. He *was* from another century. He had to be, and it was the face July had always imagined when Doyle wrote of the Baker Street Irregulars, the street waifs Holmes hired to help him. Hadn't he always imagined some child just about that size and just about that dirty? That child, in fact, had led him here to this bookshop for a purpose. July thought it might have something to do with the book the man had just mentioned.

"How much is that book you were just talking about?" he asked.

"Let's see here—three pounds will do it." July had just enough left over from his birthday money to make the purchase.

16

The House on Devonshire Place

" 'DOYLE'S NEXT HOME was in a quiet neighborhood in Marylebone, where the young writer first began his work on the Sherlock Holmes stories. The house was an ideal place to set up his practice, as well, situated on Devonshire Place, at the end of Wimpole Street.' " July looked up from the book he was reading aloud to Liberty. "Wimpole Street? Devonshire Place? Liberty, that's this house! The mews is the stable for Doyle's house!"

Elementary!

The word hung silently in the air between them. They both turned toward the corner where the ceiling dropped down below the eaves. The voice was back! But they were not spooking each time now. Slowly Liberty and July had begun to adjust to these interruptions that sounded like dim echoes from long ago.

"That house on Devonshire Place is taller than ours, isn't it?" Liberty asked.

"Yes. But we back right up to it," July said, still looking at the corner.

"In other words," Liberty said, "we share a wall." July nodded. "And," continued Liberty, "our attic must come out just about at their second floor. This was probably not really an attic at all, but a hayloft for the horses."

"Yes!" said July suddenly, his eyes scanning a page in the book. "And listen to this: 'Doyle turned his consulting room on the second floor into a writing room. Every day he would shut himself in and focus upon his work—writing through the greater part of the afternoon.' "

The twins' heads turned toward the shared wall.

"I've got to go outside and see what the roofline of this house is like," Liberty announced. She was taking no chances. She wanted to get a picture in her head of how these houses came together.

Both twins knew they would have to re-examine, inch by inch, that corner of the attic, or the loft, as Liberty now preferred to call it. Indeed there was so much to keep in their heads—house designs, theories of vanishing twins, glow-in-the-dark jelly-bean stains, the beefeater, the candles, and that strange little boy threading his way through the streets and underground of London. So much to think about, and so little time. Less than they realized. For everything seemed to come between them and their intended investigation.

"I can't believe you could have forgotten that your mother is coming this afternoon!" Zanny stood flabbergasted in the garden room. Molly and Charly had just finished feeding the fish.

If the attic had become a world to Liberty and July, the garden-room pool had become one to Charly and Molly. They had discovered that the leaves of the water lilies were so strong they could actually hold things up. So they had gone to a shop on Marylebone Street and bought tiny china animals that weighed less than an ounce each to put on the broad, green leaves of the floating plants. Their first purchase had been a small, bright green frog. Then they had bought a little kitten. As a special treat, Zanny had bought them a tiny china thatched cottage. Their dad had found another little house and a figure of an elf. The garden pool was beginning to look like a small floating village.

The smaller twins now crouched by the pool on their knees, watching the fish swim under and around this floating world. They spent hours playing here. It had become a kind of water dollhouse to them. They managed it all, filled it with characters and scenery, then stage directed the action, except for the fish, of course. It was their world, and they were the bosses. They were saving their money now to buy one more water lily so they could expand their floating village. They had seen a little china castle and a fairy princess with wings.

"We didn't really forget exactly," Liberty was saying rather lamely. "It's just . . ."

"It's just that she'll be here in less than two hours, and it's her birthday."

"Oh gee!" Both Liberty's and July's mouths dropped. There was no denying that. They had forgotten that their mother was arriving on her birthday.

"Yes! Don't you remember? And we're going to Stratford-upon-Avon, Shakespeare's birthplace, because that's what your mom wanted to do for her birthday. And your parents are going to see a Shakespeare play, which will be too long for Charly and Molly, but you'll find it interesting. We're staying at a charming old inn called the Rose and Crown. It's very hard to get into, and your dad made reservations weeks ago."

"You mean we're not going to be here tonight?" July asked, dumbfounded.

"No. That's what I just said."

"What about tomorrow night?" Liberty asked almost fearfully.

"No. They have reservations for two nights because your mom really wants to see *A Midsummer Night's Dream* and *Richard III*."

"What are those?" Liberty asked.

"Shakespeare plays! For goodness' sakes, you *have* heard of William Shakespeare, you two? Haven't you?" Zanny could not imagine what was wrong with the older twins. They had been acting very odd lately.

17

Stratford-upon-Frustration

All our plans squashed! Telepathic images were sprinting across Liberty's brain.

You see one of these old inns, you've seen them all, July flashed.

And can you believe how boring that play was? I mean, if A Midsummer Night's Dream *is what they called funny four hundred years ago, you kind of wonder how they got from that to Monty Python.*

Yeah, come to think of it, why can't we at least be at a Monty Python festival instead of this dumb Shakespeare festival—boring!

Zanny gave them a severe look. She had a feeling that the *B*-word, as in *B*-for-boring, was hovering in the air. They were sitting in the pub room of a sixteenth-century inn having a plowman's lunch, which consisted of coarse bread, cheese, and something that looked like liverwurst. The children all hated this lunch, but it was better than anything else on the menu.

"They should learn how to make squishy white bread in this country," Charly was saying. "But I'll eat this because I know it's healthy for me and will help me grow up strong."

"Yes," chimed in Molly, "I'm even going to eat the patty."

"Pâté," Zanny corrected, referring to the slice of liver pâté on their plates. She smiled. "Yes, while you're living in a foreign country it is nice to try and broaden your tastes."

"Yes." Charly nodded sagely. "That's what we're doing, broadening our tastes."

Could you throw up or what? Liberty flashed.

Miss Goody-two-shoes.

Goody-four-shoes.

Charly and Molly were laying it on thick. They had sensed that something was making their older brother and sister distant and difficult. They also knew Zanny was slightly annoyed with July and Liberty. As so often happens in a family when one child is being stubborn or difficult, the other becomes extra good.

Zanny looked at the little twins now as they so sweetly spoke of health and broadening their tastes. She knew exactly what they were doing, and she didn't trust the situation at all. As far as she was concerned there were four children that she was in charge of when the parents were not around, and something was up! She wasn't sure what it was, but it could mean trouble—two pairs of twins, each pair not only different but each individual child very different. Therefore, it was not merely two pairs of twins adding up to four kids. It was instead the square of the sum of the pairs. The square of a number is that number times itself. So it was four times four. It was, in short, as Liberty liked to say, double trouble squared.

18

The Night of the Charged Particles

THEY COULD NOT have returned to Number 3, Devonshire Mews fast enough for Liberty and July's taste. It was rainy, late in the evening, and past everyone's bedtime. Everybody was tired, and they groggily made their way to bed, some without brushing their teeth or even washing their faces. Everyone was asleep within a half hour after their return. Everyone, that is, except for July and Liberty Starbuck, who were not sleepy at all. Their mood was as wild as the weather. The soft drizzle they had driven home in had escalated into a pounding rain, and a huge smoky thunderhead blotted out the moon. Soon the London sky outside their attic window was veined with the crackle of lightning.

They had pretended to go to sleep. And Liberty had crept downstairs to check, worried that perhaps the thunderstorm might keep the family awake. But she could tell that the house slept. She knew her family well, and she had a sense of these things. Her ear was as finely attuned to the sounds of sleep, at least the sleep of her own family, as a conductor's to the instruments of his orchestra. She could pick out the music of true deep sleep in each member of her family in the same way a conductor can hear the different parts that build a chord. Now, as Liberty mounted the attic stairs once more, she knew that her family slept deeply.

When she entered the room, July was standing barefoot in his pajamas by the desk. The new jelly beans they had set out before they had left for Stratford-upon-Avon were gone. The speckled band of tape was more mottled with color than ever. Lightning now flashed in the room, illuminating it with the frenzied, pulsating light of a disco. But there were no dancers. Just two fragile-looking children in their nightclothes with their large, luminous gray eyes, pale freckled faces, and somber brows slashed with jet black bangs.

Long zigzags of white blazed in the sky. The massive clouds, heavy and dark at their bases, had spread and were flattened on top by the wind, which had grown stronger. Long and sharkish, the clouds streaked through the turbulent sky. July was mesmerized by the display. He knew how to judge the distance of the storm center by counting the seconds between the flash of lightning and the boom of thunder. A five-second gap equaled a mile. But now the gaps were two and three seconds apart. Liberty's attention was not on the electrical storm outside their window but on the storm in her head as she watched the corner of the room that shared a wall with the house that had once been Doyle's. She stared at the eaves. She was imagining. She was visualizing. She was straining every nerve, and tonight she felt the presence.

But July kept watching the clouds that were circling, schooling like predatory fish now, discharging their enormous electrical burden that shattered the sky. The time between the flash and the thunder was growing shorter, which meant that the center of the storm was coming closer. There were no more seconds to count, only slivers of seconds, between the flash of the lightning and the boom of the thunder. He knew all about thunderheads and storm clouds. He knew how the top layer attracts the strong positive electrical charge while the middle and bottom layers begin with mostly negative charges. He knew how through a process called induction—No, Watson, not deduction—the ground below the cloud becomes very strongly charged, sometimes even causing people's hair to stand on end. He knew how ice crystals could form in electrical storms, even in the summertime, and upon collision become negatively charged while the air around them became positively charged. These crystals would then drop and melt as negatively charged rain. And he knew that with each second all around them the air was heavy with zillions and zillions of collisions from charged particles. Something was going to happen.

There's more than just seams there. All the walls and the ceiling have the same space between the seams where the wall covering was taped. But there is another line starting at the base where the wall meets the floor. We were always looking at the ceiling before.

Ceiling . . . what . . . tape . . . I can't read you. Too many particles . . . air too charged.

Charged? Pres . . . ence

The telepathic communication between the twins was breaking up and became too racked with static for good transmission. They had just begun to talk out loud when suddenly there was a huge clap of thunder, and the sky flashed at the same time. A white energy seared the attic. The speckled band glowed like a gemstone serpent.

"I see it!" wailed Liberty.

July spun around, his heart skipping a beat. Then from the corner there was the terrible sound—the soft hissing, like a small jet of steam escaping, the same kind of soft hissing that Julia Stoner must have heard before the deadly swamp adder struck.

19

The Hidden Door

BUT IT WAS NOT the hiss of a swamp adder that July heard. It was the sound of tape being peeled off the wall by his sister.

"We're so stupid," Liberty was saying. "We were always looking up, up toward the ceiling and not down." She was on her knees, crouched in the corner under the eaves. The tape she was lifting revealed a seam in the plasterboard that was at an odd interval in comparison to the other seams. But it did appear to lead up toward the eaves. "When that last flash of lightning lit up the room I just happened to be looking down. They got a little sloppy here, and I could see the bulge." July was now down on his knees beside her.

Within ten minutes they had untaped a three-foot-square area on the wall just beneath the eaves. They removed two pieces of plasterboard and were now looking at what appeared to be very old laths, thin narrow strips of wood that were joined together to make a support structure for the plasterboard.

"Look, they're damp," July said. "Rain must be getting in here."

"Of course!" Liberty said. A picture of the rooflines flashed in her mind. She remembered their distinctive profile from when she had gone out to the sidewalk a few days before to look at the houses, the mews, and the big house on Devonshire Place.

Roofs.

Right. They join at a funny angle.

The water must pool where they come together.

"You would have thought they would have done a better job of refinishing."

"Quick and dirty. Probably didn't have the time to replace all these little wood pieces." July pulled out pieces of the lath. They came out easily. "Look, they put in a little insulation back there. But it's getting rotten, too, from all the dampness." He pulled out some wadded stuffing that looked like heavy coarse cotton.

"What's behind it there?" Liberty asked.

"What do you mean?"

"Look." She pulled out more of the insulation material. There was a panel of wood. The wood was in much better shape than the laths, just a crack or two.

"Well, the insulation must have done some good here," July was saying.

"Look, Jelly Bean! Those aren't cracks. They're too even. This is a small door."

"Oh, my gosh! You're right, and look—there are more of the jelly-bean stains." Indeed, around one of the cracks there was a cluster of Day-Glo bean-shaped spots. What in the world could it be? How had the jelly-bean stains gotten to this point from the tape on the desk?

Both twins' hands were on the small panel door when it moved slightly under their touch. They looked into one another's eyes searchingly. The lightning and thunder had let up. Telepathic channels were clearing.

Should we push it all the way?

I don't know. Do you think there's a snake in there?

I haven't heard any hissing sounds.

It's creepy.

I know.

Maybe if we just push a little bit together.

They put their hands together, overlapping one on top of the other, and pushed. The door swung open. The light was dim, but peering through they saw a space no bigger than a small closet and no smaller than a large cupboard. It was dusty with cobwebs, but in the dim light they could see another small door opposite the door they had just opened.

Inside, between the two doors, was a package wrapped in heavy cloth.

Their hands were drawn to the package like iron filings to a magnet. They did not even pause to ask should we or could we, for they knew that it was for this package that they had been brought, summoned, convened, signaled to these mews. It was not by accident that they had found their way to Number 3, Devonshire Mews, but indeed by design. And the design was about to be unveiled, the skein of the mystery unraveled, the shadows lightened, and the meaning revealed.

The twine of the package unknotted easily, and they unfolded the darkened canvas. Within the canvas was another layer of heavily oiled paper wrapped around something. Its seams were sealed with sealing wax, dark maroon wax the color of wine. They broke the seals and opened the paper.

"It's writing," July whispered.

"Pages and pages of it," Liberty said, lifting one and then another.

20

The Return of the Vanished Twin

" 'AND THEN my twin dropped to his knees, his face blanched with terror, his hands groping at his throat. Suddenly, in a voice I'll never forget, he gasped, "The band! The speckled band!" ' " Liberty was reading from the pages they had found in the package.

The handwriting was small, almost flat along the bottom as if the writer were using a ruler to keep the lines even. It was quite legible. She read on. " 'I glanced at my own twin, Shadrach. His pale, plump fingers nervously twisted his flowered cravat, but his eyes never left the face of the dead man, Harry Stoner. As he listened to the chilling tale, I could feel his horror for we, too, knew the subtle links that bind two souls which are so closely allied. Within the next few minutes Mr. Henry Stoner would tell us of the links that bound him to his twin brother. But for now Shadrach remained fixed, his keen mind, his uncanny powers of induction at work as he observed this gentle but weary man whose haggard expression was wrought by fear and sleepless nights.' "

They took turns reading the tale as it went on for several pages. " 'I took a step forward. In an instant the man's cap began to move, and from the dead man's hair reared the squat diamond-shaped head and puffed neck of a loathsome serpent. It writhed toward the dead man's hand and a bowl of the most lustrous pearls ever to be seen in Christendom. . . .' "

Now Liberty read the conclusion of the story. " ' "I had," said Shadrach, "come to an entirely erroneous conclusion, which shows, my dear Sherlock, how dangerous it may be to reason with insufficient data. I can only claim the merit that I instantly reconsidered my position and corrected myself in midcourse. The danger which threatened Henry Stoner and killed his brother Harry came not from the window or the door, but from the bell rope and ventilator. A ventilator that does not ventilate and a bell rope with no bell. Both could only serve as a bridge for something passing through the hole to the bed. And, of course, the ventilator served as a safe hiding place for the jewels as well.

" ' "I suppose in one sense then I am indirectly responsible for the death of Henry Stoner's uncle, Bartholomew Sholto, by driving the snake back through the ventilator. I cannot say that the death of a murderer, however, and a man of such monumental greed that he would kill his own nephew weighs very heavily on my conscience." ' " Liberty paused. "The end. And it is signed A. Conan Doyle. 1887."

"That is so weird!" July said as Liberty put down the last page. "Shadrach Holmes!"

Precisely!

There was a deep sigh. Liberty and July stared at one another.

Did you say that?

No, did you?

> *Of course not, you fools! I spoke, me, Shadrach Holmes, creation of the great author Sir Arthur Conan Doyle. You are the first aside from Doyle ever to see my name in writing. But the story in which I appeared was altered. Doyle cut me out after that first draft. In the rewrite there was never a mention of me. So my name sank into oblivion, never to be spoken, never to be read, gone forever—until you two came along.*
>
> *I thought it would take you forever to actually say my name. You see the rules of this business are such that the literary ghost's name must be spoken aloud before he or she can materialize. By speaking the name you invoke the literary ghost, or rather literary stillborn—I prefer that term. It is a more apt description of our shadowy existence, languishing in unpublished manuscripts and first drafts. In any case, as I was saying . . .*

Are you talking to us, in our heads? Liberty asked.

> *Yes, my dear. Would you prefer for me to speak out loud? I can do that, too.* The voice suddenly shifted from inside their heads and could be heard within the room. "Please choose. Either way suits me. I can speak aloud or within telepathic channels. I'm quite fluent both ways. Choose your mode and then we'll get on with it. Why? Why, you ask? How can I enter into your communication channels?"

J. B. had barely thought the question before Shadrach was answering it telepathically.

> *I, too, was a twin, although briefly. Still, it counts. You learn quickly when you live in a manuscript even if it's only a first draft. And as you well know from your own experience, twins have, as my creator Doyle wrote in that manuscript you just read, mystical bonds that do allow such communication.*

"But that's between two twins of one set. How come you can get into our telepathic patterns?"

> *Well, that comes with the territory of being a ghost who was once a twin. It's the ghost part that helps me eavesdrop. Pardon the pun, but you, of course, realize that it is within these eaves that I mostly hang about. Once you have been a twin and then become a ghost, the opportunities for communicating and gathering information are endless. You and your own little sisters will be able to cross-*

communicate beautifully when you all become ghosts.

"That's not something I'm waiting for."

Yes, I know. They have such disorderly little minds, Charlotte and Amalie. The thought of cross-communicating with them is rather daunting to say the least. Are they still so keen about the press-on nails?

"Oh gee, you know about that?" Liberty was embarrassed.

Oh, yes, my dear. Well, as I was saying, Shadrach continued, *the rules of this game are as follows. If one is a literary stillborn such as myself, and that's what you call it when as a character you have only lived within the pages of a first draft or unpublished work, your name must be read aloud from that manuscript, and then*—the twins both felt an invisible finger go up in the air as one might raise a finger to call attention to a special point being made—*and then,* repeated Shadrach, *the name must also be mentioned out of the context of the work itself and instead spoken within the framework of literary critique or criticism. Samuel Johnson you're not, July. But apparently just your saying "That is so weird, Shadrach Holmes," was enough to do the trick and help me to materialize, so to speak. The more I speak, the more parts of me may appear. For now, you'll have to be content with just my voice.*

"Who's Samuel Johnson?" Liberty asked.

Who's Samuel Johnson? Dr. Johnson—you've never heard of him? Again they felt a kind of gesture stir the air. This time it was not a finger but the palm, or more precisely the heel of the palm of a hand slapping an invisible forehead in disbelief. *Don't they teach you children anything nowadays? Samuel Johnson, or Dr. Johnson, as he was known, was the great English lexicographer, critic, and author of the last century, or rather two centuries ago if we count back from your time rather than mine. And he would have had a bit more to say about my literary existence than "That is so weird, Shadrach Holmes." Do they do nothing to develop your vocabulary a bit more in your schooling?*

"We have *Wordly Wise,*" Liberty said.

Wordly Wise? Shadrach paused. *What's that?*

"It's this kind of workbook. It's got lots of vocabulary and stuff and you write sentences and fill in blanks with the new words."

Fill in blanks. There was a definite note of disbelief in his voice. *They think children can learn syntax and narrative and story form by filling in blanks? As far as I can ascertain,* Mr. *Wordly Wise is only wise to a few words—words such as "weird" and "boring." Do you have any idea how many times you children say those words every day? You know they would do much better giving you real books to read rather than this* Wordly Wise *chappy. Well, enough about that. We have work to do.*

"We do?" both children asked at once.

Of course. You don't want me to have to remain a literary stillborn, forever doomed to this purgatorial existence of being dead but never having really lived, do you? I mean, when you see on a tombstone the words Rest in Peace it is assumed that the person has laughed and played and worked and loved in life. In short, has had a complete life. And because of this, they can rest in peace. It is the same for literary ghosts or stillborns. There is no rest for us until we've had our lives, until our place in literary history is recognized, even if only on a crumpled piece of paper thrown into a wastebasket. To be recognized that we served in a humble way as a testing ground. For that is really what a first draft is—a sketch pad for trying things out. It's exciting to see what could have been, and it helps readers understand more about what is now. My case, of course, is particularly poignant—if I do say so myself.

"Why is that?" July asked.

It's a bit of a long story.

"We want to hear," both twins said. They were now staring at a soft rose-colored glow that seemed to be lighting the corner of the eaves that was the source of the voice.

Oh, you're beginning to see my cravat and waistcoat, I believe. Yes, you see, the more I talk the more visible I become. Not totally, you understand. Just a kind of colored, fuzzy outline. Some of my garments come through quite nicely. The body remains rather illusory. But that's all right, for Doyle described me as being rather flabby, and as for my complexion, well, swine pink would be the best description of it.

We were not, Sherlock and I, supposed to be identical twins—just fraternal. It was okay with me that he was better looking, because at the start Doyle did give me all the brains. So I was willing to relinquish the dark good looks and sharp features to Sherlock. But you can imagine what a low blow it was when I found myself being cut totally out of the action, then left in this sort of undistinguished physical form, while Sherlock gets, along with all the good looks, the brains and the fame. I would have settled for a Watsonish role. I don't have to be the main character. I didn't have to be good looking and solve all the crimes. I would have played second fiddle.

And by the way, in that first draft you read you'll notice I was the one who played the violin, not Sherlock. Always in the other stories, the ones that followed, there's old Sherlock plucking out some ditty on that decrepit Stradivarius violin. Well, as you read in that first draft, he was supposed to be tone-deaf. I was the twin with the musical talent. And as for Sherlock's famous "The game is afoot!" That was originally my expression, as you can see on page fifteen. Of course it was said somewhat in jest. I was a bit of a punster, and when I accidentally knocked the chess set over and it fell on my brother's foot I said, "Drat, the game is afoot!" Conan Doyle subsequently gave the expression to Sherlock, and it has become associated with him ever since. It has been taken up by people all over the world to signify the intensity of building action, suspense. If people only knew its humble beginnings! Oh, but I'm jumping ahead in my story.

"But wait," Liberty said. "Were you ever a baby?"

A *baby*? His voice rolled with incredulity. Disbelief seemed to pour out of the very air. *Why in heaven's name would Doyle waste time making me a baby when I could come all grown-up?*

"But how did you learn to play the violin or learn who this Samuel Johnson guy was, and all the other stuff that you say we don't know?"

Well, I just did. That's part of being a character, even one that never makes it out of the first draft.

You arrive complete, in one sense. You don't have to do any growing up. You are the age you are. You do have to do some growing in.

"Growing in?" both the children asked at once.

You have to grow into the story, thread your way nimbly through the plot, become believable in terms of the historical period in which the story is set, and, most important of all, you must always be convincing.

This was not graffiti, Liberty thought, remembering what she had said about Sherlock being just a character in a novel when they had first arrived in London and had gone to Baker Street. She had wondered then what it had really meant to be a character.

You cannot look like a puppet manipulated and controlled by other forces, even if that is the case. Of course the irony of this is that you are controlled by The Great Other, the author. When a writer's words begin to lift off a page, when his imagination begins to spill over into another dimension because of the gritty reality of the world and the characters he constructs, then his characters start to live and breathe. And really, I think it's a great compliment for a person to be interesting or unusual enough to be considered a "real character." And when one is referred to as having great integrity and moral conviction we say he has "character."

"Did you ever want to be anything more than just a character in a first draft?"

> *Oh it might have been nice, but the truth is I just want to be recognized for what I was in that first draft. That is honor enough. You see how odd it is? How when you want to say that another human being is unique, full of life in the best sense of the word, the unit of comparison is taken from the world of books—"a character," a person drawn in the imagination of the writer who then goes on to live in that of the reader. It has been said that Sherlock Holmes is "a gentleman who never lived—and who will never die." That is the ultimate immortality for a literary figure. But at least Sherlock can rest. You don't see him knocking about in the eaves of this old house.*

"Are there other literary stillborns like you?"

> *Oh yes—scores of them. Authors create and throw out characters willy-nilly before they ever finally develop one that lasts for them.*

"What about those, are they unhappy, too?"

> *Yes, yes, plenty of them running around London.*

"That man!" Liberty and July both blurted at once.

> *What man?* Shadrach asked, his voice suddenly tense with suspicion.

"A man we saw in Pinchin Lane."

"Then he showed up at the Tower of London"—Liberty swallowed. Her voice was trembling, and her eyes were bright with fear—"He's one of them, isn't he?"

Yes, yes and a troublesome bloke at that. He's one of many, and he does threaten my case.

"Your case?" Liberty asked. But Shadrach ignored the question. He rushed headlong into a discussion of literary ghosts around the world.

I understand that between Pushkin and Tolstoy in Russia one can barely move without bumping into literary stillborns. All of them restless like myself, never having lived and unable to die unless they meet up with someone like yourselves who can help.

"Us? Help you?" July asked.

"Will we have to go to Russia, too, for Push-What and the other guy?"

No, no, you wouldn't be suitable for them, but for me you are.

"How?"

Be patient! I do not want to jump ahead in my story. It is essential that you understand as much as possible before you begin your mission. I must tell you more about the manuscripts, these first drafts that you have finally found.

21

The World According to Shadrach

So you see, what he was trying to do in this manuscript you discovered was combine two stories. He didn't realize it at the time, but what he was writing in the year 1887 was a first draft for both "The Adventure of the Speckled Band" and The Sign of Four.

It was much too ambitious. But this is a fault shared by many beginning writers. They try to take on the world, try to pack in too much. Snakes, jewels, the chase on the Thames, bell ropes, ventilators—it's all too much. And many parts, as you can tell, were overwritten, excessive. One might even say florid in the descriptions. We lose our grasp of not only the plot but the characters.

If indeed he had limited the scope of his plot I could have been saved. But he became overwhelmed when he went back and read this first draft. Twin detectives, twin victims, countless plots and subplots. So he threw me out entirely, despite the fact that he had planned for months—over a year in fact—to have a twin detective team.

He kept the twin victims but changed them to women. They went from Henry and Harry Stoner to Julia and Helen Stoner. In The Sign of Four *he reintroduced twin men—Thaddeus and Bartholomew Sholto. Bartholomew Sholto, if you recall, in the first draft you read aloud, was the wicked uncle. Everybody got to be somebody except me!*

Shadrach said this rather huffily, and the children could see the tassels on his cap shake a bit. There was no head, but the cap had materialized as he spoke. It was a tasseled maroon velvet smoking cap favored by gentlemen of the Victorian period. There was also a waistcoat that seemed transparent, despite being heavily brocaded. The cravat shimmered with a design of misty roses.

Well, to be fair, everybody did not get to be somebody except me. And that is why you are having trouble now with the bloke down on Pinchin Lane.

"What do you mean?" July said. A shiver started up both the twins' spines.

Well, that fellow has indeed been a villain in more first drafts than any character imaginable—but the problem is he is too obviously evil. So naturally Doyle wound up cutting him. The bloke was furious. He desperately wants to be a full-fledged literary villain, but he hasn't really got the stuff like

Professor Moriarty, Sherlock's archenemy. And what hasn't been crossed out in old manuscripts is so atrociously written that he comes off as almost comic. If there is one thing a villain doesn't like, it's to be laughed at. If you go back and read the crossed-out parts of the manuscript you have now you shall see—the bloke is a complete idiot. The writing is so awful Doyle had to run his pen through it. And rightfully so. This fellow . . . I can never remember his name—Mortley or Morttuck, but definitely not Moriarty; Doyle was always changing his name—in any case, the bloke does not want anyone to see what a truly rotten villain he makes. It is not in his interests to have this particular manuscript see the light of day. That is why you are going to have to operate with extreme caution when the time comes.

"You mean he might try to interfere, to do something to us?"

Precisely. And he is a master of deception, oddly enough. He's picked up a lot from other characters, having resided often, even if briefly, in so many first drafts.

July squirmed uncomfortably. "What about Mycroft, Sherlock's older brother? Doyle talks about him in the stories," July asked.

Him? The voice was drenched in disdain. *Listen, being a literary stillborn is bad enough, but being*

Mycroft would be worse. I'd rather be a villain in literature than that stuffy old Mycroft sitting around all day in his darned club or those little rooms he rented over in Pall Mall, never venturing from this orbit. Oh yes, occasionally he'd go over to his brother Sherlock's. So sedentary, so dull. Enough to put any reader to sleep. No, they say being a literary ghost is a fate worse than death, but I do believe I'd settle for this rather than Mycroft's lot.

They talked on through the night and into the cool gray hours of the summer dawn. Shadrach was a great talker, and by the time the sun had risen, his waistcoat, cravat, trousers, and dress pumps were fully visible. Both the children sensed that Shadrach could have made more of his physical body present, but he had chosen not to do so.

What Shadrach had chosen to do was to give them as much information as possible, not just about himself and his brief appearance in the pages of a first draft early in the career of Sir Arthur Conan Doyle, but about how the whole course of the written adventures of Sherlock Holmes, the greatest detective in literature, could have been drastically different.

"It's kind of like trying to imagine what might have happened if dinosaurs had not disappeared. Would people have happened?" Liberty said, musing.

"Evolved," J. B. offered.

Oh, Darwin, Charles Darwin! Shadrach exclaimed. *The great scientist! You realize we were born in the midst of that marvelous period. Indeed Doyle was born in the very year that Darwin published his great work* The Origin of the Species. *You might imagine the appeal of a book like that, in which through observation and deduction Darwin proposes that the earth must be a lot older than Biblical time would suggest, and that species, living things, had not always been what they appeared to be but had changed over the course of time.*

Yes, Liberty and July, I rather like your comparison of my existence to that of the dinosaurs. What might have happened if they had not all died off? It wouldn't have given us mammals, literary or living, much of a chance, would it have, now?

"Guess not," Liberty said.

So what might have happened if it had been me, Shadrach, instead of Sherlock? I merely raise the question, but I am glad to see that you children are thinking in such sweeping historical terms—because that is the kind of thinking it is going to take to get these drafts to the public and fully appreciated. This is a very serious problem, and unless resolved I shall spend my eternity in a terrible kind of limbo. You must first have your ducks in order, so to speak. Be totally prepared.

But still Shadrach seemed to avoid the question of what, precisely, the children would be required to do.

> *This first draft that you read, which later became two separate stories, "The Adventure of the Speckled Band" and* The Sign of Four, *he continued, despite being overly ambitious, was, as you can see, quite literate and well punctuated—no misspellings, even. It has some very nice language, actually much less stilted than some of his other adventures. The description of the snake's descent through the ventilator and down the bell rope is brilliant.*

Shadrach was now evidently pacing the floor, for his waistcoat, cravat, and pumps seemed to be swinging back and forth in a small arc between the eaves and the window. He did this in much the same manner as a lawyer would pace back and forth in a courtroom when trying to convince a judge and jury of a client's innocence.

"But how come Doyle cut you out entirely?" Liberty asked. "It seems kind of unfair."

"Raw deal, I'd say," July added.

"I mean you didn't . . ." Liberty's thought dwindled off.

> *I know what you're thinking, my dear—what could Shadrach Holmes, fraternal twin to Sherlock, have done to deserve such a fate?*

"Do you think Sherlock was jealous?" July offered. "Charly and Molly are always jealous of us."

"Constantly, it's really annoying," Liberty added.

Oh, it could be that, but I have also thought that perhaps Doyle himself was so vain that he did not want people to think of him as this flabby, rather unathletic-looking pink blubberball.

Liberty could not imagine an author becoming this wrapped up in a character. And Shadrach, reading her mind, replied.

You cannot pry apart the creator from the character he has created after a certain kind of bonding takes place on the page. It does not matter that they may not be identical. In the author's mind they share a kind of spirit despite their differences.

You know Doyle was terribly proud of his physical prowess. Stood over six feet tall, weighed in at seventeen stone—that's over two hundred pounds in your measure, I believe. A great cricket player. Twice took all ten wickets in an inning. Played football—what you call soccer, I believe—into his forties. Boxed and was one of the first people ever to go skiing. He went when he was in Switzerland and some Swiss mountaineer guides had just invented the sport of sliding down mountains on boards.

"One thing"—Liberty had a sudden thought—"Do you mind if I ask, I mean seeing as you have already said you're sort of plump?"

Oh, go right ahead. Don't be afraid. I'm the first to admit that I am not a grand physical specimen.

"Well, are you the one who's been eating our jelly beans?"

Ah yes, I simply could not resist. They've become quite a habit with me, particularly the pink ones. An addiction, one might say. Although I don't use that term lightly, for as you know my brother Sherlock had a serious cocaine problem.

"Yes," July said. "But one thing, how do you eat if you're a ghost?"

Gastrospiration, Shadrach answered.

"What?" both Liberty and July asked at the same time.

Gastrospiration, he repeated. *You've heard of expiration?* The children nodded. *And transpiration and perspiration and inspiration?* They again nodded. *Well, gastrospiration is how ghosts eat. It's a vaporization and distillation process by which the food, in this case jelly beans, disappears or is consumed, but not by the normal biological process. We cannot gastrospirate everything, nothing too complex, only the simplest sort of molecular structures—and what are jelly beans but a lot of sugar and glycerin and color? I cannot digest the color though; hence the pastel puddles left behind. We call this bioluminescence. The colors of my cravat and waistcoat are another example of bioluminescence. I think of it as remnants of the visible magnetic energy that is left from a product, or a living thing for that matter. I dabbled somewhat in physics, you know. Sherlock was more interested in chemistry.*

But getting back to me and my love of candy. You see, that's one difference, small but nonetheless significant, between me and Sherlock. He tended toward a sparse and I might say monotonous diet. The chop and all those overcooked vegetables for which we English are famous washed down with a glass of claret. Rarely did he take pudding, or dessert as you call it, while I myself could have made entire meals out of puddings and skipped those horrid limp vegetables. However, I gained no pleasure from cocaine. Think now how different the course of Holmes's adventures might have been if instead of cocaine, he had been addicted to candy?

"Candy can make you hyperactive," Liberty offered. "You should see Charly and Molly after they eat a lot of candy. They're bouncing off walls."

Well, there you go, Shadrach said. *I don't think I would have bounced off walls, in spite of being so portly.* He chortled. *But things might have come out much differently.*

"So Doyle didn't want to be like you?" July asked.

No. I don't really think he would have wanted to be a cocaine addict either. But there is no use mincing words about it. I just didn't have the appeal for him that Sherlock did. But not only that. He didn't want to have to spread out the glory, or have twin detectives share it. And there was always, of course, the slight disdain for my kind of thinking—inductive, as opposed to deductive. Inductive is the kind of thinking that we associate with intuition, emotion, leaps of faith if you will, as opposed to the deductive variety, Sherlock's specialty, which is thought of in terms of cold, dispassionate logic. But I notice that you two induce very nicely. And I'll wager that some of the best problem solving in the world is done by utilizing both kinds of thinking.

"Yeah," July said. "Liberty's much better at keeping whole pictures in her head. She can remember the shapes of things. She really helped me draw in the map of the Great Lakes in a geography test we had."

"But July's better at remembering little things—like the capital of Minnesota."

The Twin Cities, Shadrach said.

"You knew that?" both twins said with surprise.

I told you that I arrived all grown-up—that means a working knowledge of geography. But getting back to these two kinds of thinking.

"Yes?" Liberty asked.

Well, Doyle only wanted one style of thinking and one type of detective, and that detective became Sherlock. But that is why it is such luck that you have moved in here, you two who combine these two ways of thinking, and that is why I have been going on so long about all this. For you children will need all the information possible if you are to succeed in your mission. I have been waiting over a century for something like this to happen. What luck.

"But it wasn't luck, exactly," July said. He remembered the long, cool shadow that Sherlock's head cast on the wall of his bedroom back in Washington. And Liberty remembered the echoes pressing her from sleep at dawn on that morning, which now seemed so long ago.

"No, it didn't seem that way to us. We were sort of drawn here," Liberty added. Briefly, the children told Shadrach about what had happened after their strange journey to Pinchin Lane and how they had found the house in the mews.

Very interesting, Shadrach sighed when the children finished their story. *And you know that horrid man in Pinchin Lane is not only a failed literary villain, but he was cruel to animals as well. He was much more successful as an animal abuser than as a murderer—if that is any comfort to you.*

"Not really," Liberty replied.

"But how come we could see him, and we couldn't see you?" July asked.

Oh, quite simple. If you do have the good luck to make it into a second draft you may become visible on occasion. And he did once make it into a second draft. But believe me, I would rather be invisible and remain in a first draft than ever be cruel to animals.

Liberty and July nodded in solemn approval.

And you see, Toby, the dog, was supposed to be another breed. So this is a case where you have both a man and a dog running about, exiles from a second draft, literary stillborns nonetheless. But one cannot be all things to all characters, and in the case of the man on Pinchin Lane and that horrible Doberman there is no existing manuscript, so unless one is written in which these characters are used, these literary ghosts cannot be put to rest.

Liberty shuddered as she remembered the foam from the dog's mouth scalding her cheek. Shadrach noticed this, and she almost felt something like a pat on her head.

No need to fear, my dear. It's me they're really interested in, not you. That fellow on Pinchin Lane could cause me some problems—he'll do anything to prevent this draft from being published, to stop it before the whole world sees what an awful character he is. They might try to use you to get to me. But it's not exactly fatal when you're already a ghost, you know.

"But I'm not a ghost—yet," Liberty said in a small whisper.

"But what about the little boy, the one who led me to that shop—The Bow Street Runners?" July asked.

> *Ah ha!* said Shadrach. *Now that is another story.*

They felt the phantom finger punctuate the air.

"He was a Baker Street Irregular, wasn't he? Like one of the little street children that would help Sherlock get information," Liberty asked now.

> *He was almost a Baker Street Irregular. Again cut in a first draft. I believe it was a first draft of* A Scandal in Bohemia*—the story with Irene Adler.*

"Is there any existing draft or manuscript?" July asked.

> *No, I'm sorry to report. He is a little spirit who does deserve some rest, Simon, that is.*

"Simon? Is that his name?"

> *Yes. That's all I know about him. He was just a figment of Doyle's imagination, but he did make it into several second drafts of various Sherlock Holmes tales. He never lasted longer than a split second, however, and then Doyle would just cut him.*

"Oh," July said. There was dejection in his voice.

Well, there might be a way you can help him if you can help me. That is why you must perform this mission, Shadrach offered.

"Well, what exactly is the mission?" Liberty burst out impatiently. She could stand it no longer.

You must simply do this. You must bring this manuscript, this first draft, to the attention of the world. It won't be easy. You will have to hire solicitors, lawyers as you call them. You will have to find biblio-detectives and handwriting experts. The procedures of verification and legal entitlement will be complicated, and then of course you must notify the various Sherlock Holmes societies, of which there are many all over the world. London is the center for many of them, and I would suggest that you might contact the one known as the Blue Carbuncles. However, I must warn you. There shall be difficulties with these blokes. Especially in terms of Liberty as a co-discoverer.

"What? Why? Why me?" Liberty asked.

Well. There was a deep sigh and both children could see the waistcoat expand. *They do not admit women.*

"What!" Liberty was dumbfounded. "Where are these guys from?"

The Victorian age, my dear. Straight out of it. I'm afraid they have very strict rules about the presence of women at their meetings. It is strictly forbidden.

"I don't understand." Liberty was absolutely bewildered.

It's very difficult, I admit, and I, after all, am a Victorian, but I've learned a lot. However, it was the belief back then that women were lesser, weaker, not as smart, and needful of protection.

"That is the biggest bunch of malarkey I've ever heard. They're going to be needful of protection if they don't let me in," Liberty fumed.

I don't doubt it for a minute, my dear. And we shall figure out a way to work around this. For you have, both of you, discovered the manuscript through your brilliant combination of deductive and inductive reasoning, and I, for one, shall not stand placidly by while one twin gets deleted. I give you my solemn word on that, Liberty. I do think however that you might need some outside help with this. This is a tall order for you both, considering your age.

"But who would help?"

Zanny the Nanny. He said the words succinctly. He must have been fingering his watch chain now for it seemed to jingle a bit. *I must be on my way. The sun is rising, and I really prefer the night to the day.*

And with that he began to melt away—first the dress pumps, next the trousers, then the embroidered waistcoat, and finally the cravat with the roses and the little velvet smoking hat with the tassels. One tiny rose and a tassel seemed to linger for several seconds, the better part of a minute, in a shaft of the early morning sunlight, and then Shadrach was gone.

22

To Pump Court

THE WORLD APPEARED rinsed and lovely that morning, and not for one second did either Liberty or July Starbuck doubt the strange events that had transpired in the attic the previous night. Both, however, had doubts about letting Zanny in on their secret, at least at this point. After all, it was Zanny who had come up with the notion that the man from Slaughter Glen was a naturalist, or at worst just a run-of-the-mill pervert. What would she say about Shadrach, a self-described literary ghost? She would listen to them for three minutes, go take a shower, re-emerge as a super-adult, and tell them some psychological gobbledygook about their overactive imaginations. Probably take them off candy and put them on a diet of whole grains and carrot juice.

They attributed Shadrach's advice of seeking help from a grown-up to the typical kind of caution an adult would think necessary. Shadrach might be a ghost, but he was still a grown-up, even if he had only lived for a brief time within the pages of a first draft. He had been conceived by Doyle as a full-fledged adult, if not a full-fledged character. And there was a difference. So, as far as Liberty and July were concerned, Shadrach might be a literary stillborn, an unrealized character, but he was a fully operational grown-up in terms of his thinking, especially when he was thinking about children. Maybe Shadrach was right, maybe they would need help. But as soon as you got grown-ups involved, there was always the chance they might take over the whole show, even Zanny. For now, July and Liberty wanted to try it on their own.

That afternoon they went to where they remembered the solicitors, or lawyers, had their offices—to Pump Court behind Fleet Street. They took the underground from Baker Street and emerged at the Holborn station. The twins made their way past the Royal Courts of Justice and shops that specialized in the wigs and judicial robes that all solicitors were required to wear when appearing in court.

"It's enough to make you not want to be a lawyer," July said as they stopped to look at one such wig on the head of a mannequin. The coarse white hair looked more like bristles than actual hair and had been rolled into sausage shapes that lay across the back in rigid rows. A tiny braided tail hung down at the base of the wig. The bangs were shaped into the same sausagelike curls.

"Cute!" said Liberty, her voice drenched in sarcasm. "Real cute."

"Well, as long as whoever wears one can think under it. That's all we care about, right?"

"Right."

Pump Court was not a court of law but a courtyard in which solicitors had their offices. It was tucked away behind an ancient church that, according to a plaque, was built by the Knights Templar over eight hundred years before, in the twelfth century. That morning a wedding in the church was about to begin, and chords of organ music streamed out from the church. Liberty and July paused to watch. The bride stood before the arched doorway of the church, about to enter. She carried a huge bouquet of small white flowers that erupted in a frothy cascade of tiny blossoms.

Look, you can see the flowers tremble, Liberty flashed.

They're shivering, July telewhispered.

It looks like mist almost.

Mist from a waterfall.

They both wished suddenly that they were anywhere but in this quiet ancient place. The chiseled stone, rounded arches, and carefully trimmed squares of green grass were so serious, so grown-up. It was a place where laws were studied and interpreted, and promises were made for life.

Maybe Shadrach was right. Maybe we need to bring Zanny, J. B. flashed.

Well, we're here. So we might as well find ourselves a solicitor.

Every one of the brick buildings that enclosed Pump Court had a list of solicitors posted at the door, floor by floor.

How do we know where to begin? Liberty teleflashed.

Do you hear a crackling? July flashed.

I don't think so . . . why? Do you?

Just for a second there, a little sizzle . . .

No, it's broad daylight, Liberty . . . we're not in a dangerous place. This is the center for all the lawyers of London. People are at least going to be law-abiding here.

Too bad the lawyers don't list their specialties.

I wonder if there is such a thing as a lawyer who specializes in old manuscripts.

At just that moment a bewhiskered man seemed to materialize out of a little tunneled alley alongside the building.

"Can I help you?" he asked cheerily. "Looking for someone in particular?"

"Well, as a matter of fact, yes," Liberty said quickly. "We're looking for a solicitor who specializes in old documents." Almost as soon as she said it, she felt she shouldn't have. She felt she had let the cat out of the bag too soon, exposed herself. They had been careful to bring only two pages of the old manuscript, and now already this man was asking and answering questions so quickly.

"Well, I myself have had some experience in this field. Do you have the manu—er—uh document with you?"

He almost said "manuscript"!

How did he know?

You and your big mouth, Liberty!

I'm sorry!

Now the man was actually touching Liberty's elbow and moving her away from the building's entrance where they were standing. "I'm Mr. Swepstone," he said, pointing to the sign where the solicitors were listed. Sure enough, there was a Mr. Godfrey Swepstone listed. "But I'm afraid that my offices are undergoing renovations right now. A waterpipe burst last winter and left the ceiling and walls a mess. So I've taken temporary offices just a few blocks from here." He had his hand firmly on Liberty's elbow.

Good grief, it's him! And I'm being abducted. I can't believe it. Don't talk to strangers—how many times have I heard Mom and Dad say that? Always harping on it with Molly and Charly and . . . Forget Mom and Dad, think of what Shadrach told us!

By this time, the man had a hand on July's arm. "Now you say you brought the documents with you."

"No! No!" July's voice came out in an abrupt little bark. "No, I said nothing like that. No, we don't have the document at all."

"Well then, what's that you are carrying?" Harshness, mixed with impatience, had crept into Swepstone's voice. The man was eyeing the envelope. It was a thin envelope. Without even thinking, July began to fold it into a triangle. Then he turned back two of the corners to form smaller triangles.

"Now I think you should get it into your 'ead that it would be wery waluable . . ." A blizzard of *w*'s hissed through the air like wipers or vipers about to be dropped on their heads or 'eads! But above all of those *w*'s sailed the envelope with the two pages of the old manuscript. As the man was reaching out for the envelope he had let go of July's elbow. At the moment he let go, July had raised his arm and lofted his paper airplane toward the roof.

Suddenly a shriek pierced the tranquil courtyard and seemed to strip the notes of the organ music right from the air. A red tornado, full of freckles and spitting blue fire from her eyes, hurtled toward them. "Stop that instantly! Stop that man! He's kidnapping those children. Stop!"

"Zanny!" both twins cried out.

And then from the other corner of the courtyard there was a great flapping of black, like some enormous crow about to land. "Unhand those children, I say! Unhand them!"

23

Jonathan Swan, Solicitor

"MY GOODNESS! He was a slippery fellow. He just seems to have vanished into thin air." The young solicitor's wig was askew. The little pigtail hung over one ear. "I guess I don't need this on now. I'm not in court." He snatched the wig off his head and put it in a pocket of his robes. "Are you all right? He didn't harm you, did he?" They were all so completely shaken that it took them a moment to answer.

"Yes and no," Liberty and July both answered.

"I saw you," said the young solicitor. "If you'll forgive the expression, you were like a woman possessed." His eyes were riveted on Zanny and overflowing with admiration. And the children noticed something else.

Is this love? Liberty telewondered.

Could be. He looks a little moony to me. It can't all be just from relief at saving us.

Well, he's very cute. Zanny should look at him more. She seems a little out of it.

I guess this is part of being a nanny. Children first.

How boring!

"What was he doing to you? What did he want?" Zanny said.

"That!" July replied, looking up at the gutter where the envelope had fetched up in its flight to safety.

"What's that?" both Zanny and the young solicitor asked. And then, before either one could answer, Zanny said, "Does it have anything to do with Sherlock Holmes and somebody named Shadrach?" The twins were dumbfounded.

"Yes!" they both said at once.

"How did you ever know?" Liberty asked.

"It's a long story," Zanny said.

"Not as long as ours," July said.

"Perhaps we'd better go into my office. It's right here." The solicitor pointed to a name on the sign that said Jonathan Swan.

"First I have to get that envelope," July said.

"No problem," Jonathan replied. "Let me give you a leg up, and then I think you can get a purchase on that pillar and reach right into the gutter."

Five minutes later the children were sitting in Jonathan Swan's office.

"Well," he was saying, "these two pages certainly do look authentic to me. And you say that the rest of the manuscript, this draft, is back at your home in Devonshire Mews?"

"Yes," said Liberty. "We didn't want to risk bringing all of it."

"Very judicious." Jonathan nodded and then smiled. "My, my! You really have stumbled onto something! So it could have been Shadrach Holmes instead of Sherlock. Goodness! What a discovery. My congratulations to you both."

They had purposely avoided telling Jonathan about the ghost of Shadrach and the whole idea of literary stillborns. As far as Jonathan knew, they had merely found this manuscript by poking around in an old hidden closet. And the horrible man who had nearly stolen it from them was probably just somebody who had heard them on the underground and followed them. The twins, however, were consumed with curiosity about how Zanny knew to follow them here. She had evidently met up with Shadrach in some way. But they dared not ask. Liberty had put her foot down, telepathically speaking.

We can't say a word about these ghosts, if only for Zanny's sake. This guy's too cute. We don't want to blow it romantically for Zanny. We start talking about ghosts and literary stillborns and he'll think we're nuts and be off faster than you can say "speckled band"!

The procedure was simple. Jonathan agreed to represent the twins for a token sum of one pound, about two dollars. He then took an affidavit from them that constituted an official statement of where they had found the document and what they believed it to be. They were then to take these two papers, collect the rest of the manuscript from the mews, and meet Jonathan in one hour at Lloyd's of London, where the preliminary insurance documents, something he called a rider, would be drawn up.

The manuscript would then be put into a vault for safekeeping. By the next day, Jonathan would have contacted a specialist in manuscripts and antiquarian documents to evaluate the authenticity of this first draft. He would, of course, at the same time bring in a Holmesian scholar.

"How did you know?" The cab back to the mews had hardly pulled away from the curb when July and Liberty blurted out their question.

Zanny sank back against the seat of the car. "You know all those stories about people claiming to be kidnapped by extraterrestrials? You know those things you kids love reading in the supermarket checkout lines, the tabloids?"

"Don't tell me Shadrach kidnapped you?" Liberty gasped.

"Well, not exactly, but I guarantee you it was as exhausting. Here I thought I was going to have a nice restful day off. Your mother was planning to spend the whole day with Charly and Molly at that birthday party at the zoo that one of the embassy families was giving.

Well, I just couldn't relax. Something kept nudging me mentally—not really physically. But I just knew I had to go upstairs to see how you guys were. I had this feeling that something wasn't right. So I went upstairs, and I can't describe it." Zanny's eyes had a faraway look. "I felt this . . . this presence . . . an inescapable presence. It was particularly strong in one corner of the room."

"Near the eaves," July said.

"Yes, near the eaves. And it looked as if a panel had been removed and then put back into the wall."

"It had," Liberty said solemnly.

"But I was afraid to go near there."

"You were?" they both asked.

Then Liberty spoke. "You mean Shadrach came out without you reading the manuscript or saying his name?"

"I'm afraid so, and I'm afraid that it might have caused him mortal damage, if you can speak of such a thing in reference to a ghost."

"Mortal damage. Oh no!" Both twins gasped.

"Yes. You see," continued Zanny, "he manifested himself in a way that was in violation of all the rules."

"Oh no!" July wailed. "Why didn't you say his name?"

"Well, how was I supposed to know his name? I mean Shadrach is not one of those names that just pops right into your head."

"Oh dear," said Liberty. "So did you actually see him?"

"Well, sort of. There were these dim rosettes hovering in the air."

"His cravat," the twins said.

"And the more he talked," Liberty asked, "the more of him appeared, right?"

"Well, now that's the problem. You see I think it weakened him greatly to have come forth and manifest himself in this way. He took a great risk by appearing. He told me that he could not really assess the damage it had done."

"Oh no!" groaned July.

"How did it happen? How did he finally appear?" Liberty asked.

"Well, I was just up there, too scared to go into that corner but too scared to leave, and worried to death about the two of you. I think I must have started crying or something because this voice just blurted out, 'I can't stand women who cry. Stop that sniveling.' " Zanny paused, then continued. "He told me to pull myself together, and then he explained this whole thing and what you two were up to. You see, he was terribly frightened that something awful might happen, and he really cares greatly for you both. I guess he thought it was worth the risk. But showing himself to me the way he did was even riskier, and he seemed very weak when I left him."

"Oh no!" both Liberty and July cried.

"What could happen to him?" July asked.

"Yeah, how do you die twice?" Liberty asked.

"I'm not sure, but I felt it might be something worse

than being a literary stillborn. He seemed too weak to explain. But obviously if he went to this great risk he felt there was something to be gained. And if we work fast enough and get this manuscript out to the world, there's hope he might survive, if you can use that word for someone who is already a ghost."

24

Back in the Honey Pit

Look! There are those big smoochy marks again, Molly teleflashed.

It looks like a worm going headfirst into a volcano.

Oh good grief, you little twerps. Aunt Honey's gross enough without your play-by-play commentary, J. B. flashed.

Shut up. I want to hear this, guys, Liberty broke in. Ever since Shadrach had come into their lives, the cross-communication between all the twins had improved.

"Well, this is all so exciting," Aunt Honey was saying. "Who would have thought that these two . . ."

Just don't say it, Honey Buckets . . . don't say it! I just know she's going to say something about underacheivers, July. I just know it!

Cool it, Liberty, cool it. She hasn't said anything yet.

"This set, especially . . ."

See—set . . . what'd I tell you? You said it before, July, no assembly required . . .

"I mean the other set—" Honey continued. Putnam cleared his throat violently. "Honey, my dear . . ."

He's really mad. He only calls her "my dear" when he wants to call her a turkey.

"Well Put, let's be reasonable. Haven't they exceeded your expectations?"

"They've only begun, Honey, you turk—dear."

"Well, when Madeline called me and told me this splendid news I thought, I just have to come. I mean, you know . . ." She rolled her megawatt eyes around the room and tossed her scarf dramatically around her throat.

She should just strangle herself with that scarf now and save me the trouble, Liberty flashed.

The little twins almost giggled out loud.

Listen, Charly flashed, *I think she's just trying to say that me and Molly are a teeny tiny bit better, that's all.*

With therapists like you who needs crazy people? July telemuttered.

We don't get it. What's a therapist?

Never mind, you little pig droppings. Liberty, do you want the scarf now or later?

July said we were therapists. We want to know what it means. Is it something to do with press-on nails?

Was Laura Ingalls Wilder a therapist—is it good?

There was a veritable teleshouting match going on between Charly, Molly, July, and Liberty.

Hey, everybody, shut up! Here it comes. Here's your chance, Liberty, listen up!

"Well, in any case, Madeline, I thought I'd wear that creamy chiffon, it shows off my coloring, don't you know."

Don't you just know it, Honey Guts!

"And then I thought for a wrap that pink feather boa."

Constrictor? We should be so lucky, Liberty teleflashed. She then turned to Aunt Honey with her sweetest smile, the one where she bit lightly on the inside of her left cheek so her dimple winked. "Well, Aunt Honey, I hate to tell you, but they don't allow females to be present in the same room with the Blue Carbuncles when they are meeting."

"What? Why, I never heard of such a thing!"

They all nodded solemnly, almost mournfully, at Aunt Honey.

"Then I guess I can't . . ." But even Honey had the grace not to finish the thought.

The four Starbuck twins did it for her. *Wear your boa constrictor.*

"Alas!" sighed Putnam.

Try to hold yourself together, Dad; we know this is tough. And all the twins telegiggled.

25

The Blue Carbuncles

"BEAUTIFUL!"

"Incontrovertible veracity."

"A stunning revelation. Boggles, you feel this was probably finished sometime after he and Louise moved into the Marylebone house?"

"Beautiful! Beautiful!"

Five gentlemen, Liberty and July Starbuck, their father, Zanny, and Jonathan Swan were seated at a long, oval-shaped table in a paneled conference room of Lloyd's of London. Because of the absolute secrecy required, not even a secretary from the firm was in the room to take notes.

"Now we are here today presumably to decide how we shall present this landmark discovery to the world," the man named Boggles was intoning in a grave voice. "It was Dunphy's and my thought that indeed it would be most appropriate to make the announcement at the monthly meeting of the Blue Carbuncles, which will be next Wednesday. We would, of course, have a press release prepared with all due credit to the discoverers—July and Liberty Starbuck. Now there is the gender problem."

Liberty began a slow smolder. She had been prepared for this. Shadrach had been the first to inform her that the fact that she was a girl might present a problem to the Blue Carbuncles. But somehow neither she nor July nor Zanny had ever believed this would really become a hurdle, and neither had Jonathan or Putnam. But both men were prepared to put up a good fight to protect Liberty's right to be present at the momentous occasion when the children's find would be revealed to the world. "Now we all think, Miss Starbuck, that it would be a terrible shame for you not to be able to participate."

"With all due respect, Mr. Boggles," Putnam broke in, "it is unthinkable."

"Er . . . er . . ." Mr. Boggles coughed nervously. "Yes, yes, of course, Mr. Starbuck."

Jonathan shifted in his seat. He was prepared to argue on legal grounds for Liberty's rights, but he didn't want to until it was absolutely necessary. He had hoped to be able to gently convince them of Liberty's inalienable right to be present.

"The bylaws of the organization leave little doubt about such issues as female presence at meetings. Indeed, the only time women can attend is on the occasion of some of our summer outings. There is the tea in honor of the queen's birthday, Queen Victoria, that is, and women are invited to that, but really I don't think we'd want to wait until then to announce this marvelous discovery, and I'm sure Miss Starbuck would not want us to wait that long, either."

Liberty didn't answer. She glared at Mr. Boggles.

You really tick me off, you bug-eyed old Boggley bat.

Cool it, Liberty! J. B. teleflashed.

"Mr. Boggles." Jonathan Swan rose from his chair. Liberty could sense he was perturbed. Zanny looked on, her eyes brimming with admiration. Oh, they were in love all right, but Liberty was so mad at this point she didn't give a hoot.

"Yes?" Boggles looked up.

"It is my understanding that the monthly meeting of the Blue Carbuncles usually occurs at a pub, not far from here actually. And it is furthermore my understanding of English jurisprudence that under the law, children are not permitted in rooms where wine and spirits are served. So, as the case now stands, neither one of the children would be able to attend this august gathering. In my clients' best interests, I could not as their solicitor allow them to attend this meeting in the first place."

What is he getting at?

Neither one of us gets to go!

"My clients, Liberty and July Starbuck," Jonathan continued, "would be perfectly free to announce this landmark discovery on their own. And their father, Putnam Starbuck, senior attaché to Ambassador Whitmore of the Court of St. James, has informed me that Ambassador Whitmore is prepared to offer the American embassy as the site for this marvelous announcement."

"This is an outrage!" Mr. Boggles sprang from his seat. The appraiser of manuscripts, the Holmesian scholar, and the two gentlemen from the Blue Carbuncles were aghast.

"Impossible!" sputtered Mr. Ambersley-Witt. "We are dealing here with an English document, a piece of England's great literary history. Sir Arthur Conan Doyle was English, and his creation, the character of Sherlock Holmes, is English to the core! It would be a violation of the gravest order to have this announcement made in the embassy of a foreign power."

"Rather reminiscent of the Elgin Marbles," Putnam said quietly and smiled. All five men turned an uncomfortable shade of pink at Putnam Starbuck's reference to England's 1803 theft of the marble frieze from the Parthenon in Athens, Greece. It had been a very touchy subject for well over a century. The British were somewhat used to being attacked and had standard answers, but perhaps they had never had the tables turned on them so deftly as Putnam was continuing to do now.

I forgive him for the War on Fluorocarbons, Liberty flashed. *The guy's really a pro!*

"The director of acquisitions of the Smithsonian Institute in Washington, D.C., is a close personal friend of mine." Putnam was speaking almost casually now. "I am sure he would be most interested in this first draft discovered by two young Americans."

The five gentlemen looked absolutely horrified at this suggestion. One might as well have said that the Tower of London was back in business and their own grandchildren would be the first new inmates. Boggles actually reached into his breast pocket for a pill box and slipped a tablet into his mouth. "I'm sure there is some way around this," he sputtered.

"I'm sure there is," Putnam said, rising to leave. "I shall tell Ambassador Whitmore to hold off informing the press until we hear from you. That'll be tomorrow, as I think we've all agreed that we do not want to delay things unnecessarily."

"Yes, of course."

They're scared, Liberty. Look at that guy—old double name with the strawberry-shaped nose. He's quaking!

Yeah, and Boggles is getting more bug-eyed by the second.

"Of course."

There was a chorus of "of courses" and coughs and low growls that emanated from way back in the throats of the five English gentlemen.

26

Shadrach Imperiled

THE SOLUTION TO the gender problem was not altogether satisfactory, at least not from Liberty's point of view. Nor was it from Putnam's, because it did violate, albeit in a limited way, the Starbuck family motto—*Sui Veritas Primo*, Truth to Self First. However, Jonathan Swan advised them to go along with it. After all, as he pointed out, Liberty's true identity would be recognized eventually. And it was only for the evening gathering and dinner of the Blue Carbuncles that Liberty would have to disguise herself and appear in the clothes of a boy.

> *Well, well,* Shadrach was saying. He was still ailing. Only his rosettes hung dimly in the dying light of the summer evening, and Liberty did not want to burden him with her troubles. But he had appeared in this rather weakened, anemic form nonetheless. *You see, my dear, you are in the tradition of a great many literary, particularly*

> *Shakespearean, characters—heroines who disguised their sex to achieve their goals. Look at Rosalinde and Viola, for example. You have heard of these characters, haven't you?*

"Yes," Liberty lied. She did not want to tire him out with her abysmal ignorance. His obvious weakness worried them greatly. And how could she tell him that it did not matter that this Rosalinde and what's-her-name had disguised themselves as boys? They were literary figures and not flesh-and-blood humans. She was not a character. She was a living female.

> *Yes, yes, now that's a good girl.* She felt something lighter than the earliest morning breeze brush her hand. *I really think we have a chance of pulling this off.*

"Yes," Liberty said fiercely. She had to remember the goal here—liberating Shadrach from his unhappy existence. She heard him sigh, and she knew what he was thinking. They could pull it off if he could make it to the time of the announcement. He had been growing dimmer every day. Yesterday there had been three rosettes visible; the day before there were four, and now today only one. "Yes, Shadrach, I promise I'll do my best at the meeting. Zanny says no one will guess I'm a girl. I'm going to wear a deerstalker hat just like July's and Sherlock's. I guess all the members of the Blue Carbuncles wear them to these monthly meetings. So I won't have to cut my hair, just tuck it up."

Good. The word came like the whisper of a wind over dry leaves.

"And I'll wear pants and a shirt and tie, and July and I will look like absolutely identical twins."

Oh, thank you, Liberty. You know, I heard your parents talking the other night about a friend they knew back in Washington who was addicted to alcohol.

"Don't talk, Shadrach. It seems to be tiring you out. It's not strengthening your bioluminescence."

Yes, I know, but I must say this. With this person, it is sad that he is addicted to alcohol rather than life, like my brother and his cocaine habit. But then, of course, Sherlock only lived in a book, and a character in a book has no control. But this other person is real. Despite the illness he must control his own destiny, and he can control it because he is real. I'm just from the pages of a draft, an unpublished manuscript. It is my lot to be without control, although I have tried as hard as literarily possible to jump the boundaries of the page.

If that seems grossly unfair, my powerless state, perhaps it is, perhaps it isn't. But one of the few just deserts is that because I have no power I can seek a new author. In a sense you and your brother are the authors who shall re-create me for the literary world. The two of you are my choice, because you and your brother and your entire family are addicted to life. You have brought life into this house. You have brought goldfish and squabbles and china villages that float on lily pads. You are, every single member of your family, characters!

"Don't talk anymore, please, Shadrach!" Liberty's eyes focused on the dimly pulsating rosette.

But Liberty, you must now think as a character. For they have written this chapter, this stupidity about no women at the meeting. It is as if you have no control, like a literary character. But you do have power. So you must do something very subtle here. Remember when I said that a character must never look like a puppet, despite the fact that she or he has no control? You must do the same. You must not look like a puppet, but be able to thread your way nimbly through the plot of this meeting. You must fit believably into the setting, but if you are really clever you can manipulate the plot. Remember, you may look like a literary character, but you're a flesh-and-blood girl. There are still things that can be done when you are at that meeting.

Then there was a slight sibilant whisper like a stream of air trying to form a word that began with *s*. But she could not hear the word, and the last rosette had melted into the night. Had Shadrach gone forever?

There was no way of knowing. Liberty felt tears spring to her eyes. And what had he meant? How could she behave like a character and yet have the control of a real person? How was she supposed to manipulate the plot and nimbly thread her way through that meeting in her boy's clothes? And what was the last word he had started to say? Then suddenly it came to her! Why, of course. She knew precisely what to do!

27

Just Plain Me!

THE MONTHLY MEETING of the Blue Carbuncles was to be held at the Carlton Club, located on Saint James Street and founded in 1832 by the Duke of Wellington. By holding the momentous occasion in a private club rather than a publican house, or pub, the sticky issue of serving liquor on the premises with children present had been avoided. But the world Liberty and July entered when they walked through the portals of the Carlton Club was most definitely a masculine one, filled with the scent of leather and hung with paintings of blood sports.

Drooling hounds and dead animals, Liberty teleflashed to her brother. *They think that's really macho, don't they?* She nodded toward a portrait over a huge fireplace of a dead rabbit held in the mouth of a hunting dog. Blood was dripping from a gash in the rabbit's neck.

Well, I don't think Beatrix Potter would have liked it, July replied telepathically.

Most men are so stupid.

Don't look so grouchy. Here comes Boggles.

"Good evening, children. You look very nice." The remark was made to both twins, but Mr. Boggles nodded in Liberty's direction. Then he came up close to her and whispered in her ear. "Remember, you only have to keep this up for the duration of the meeting. After that you can announce yourself to the press and be given full credit as the young woman who has discovered this wonderful manuscript."

It had been announced that a new piece of Holmesian information had been discovered, and that two American children were in some way involved. Those were the only details that were given out. Only Mr. Boggles and the gentlemen who had come with him to Lloyd's of London knew that the find was a lost manscript that offered the most important insights ever into the creation of Sherlock Holmes. All these gentlemen, as well as Putnam, Jonathan, Liberty, and July, were very nervous and could barely eat a bit of the roast-beef dinner.

As the members were finishing dessert, Mr. Boggles stepped up to the podium to call the meeting to order. Liberty and July were in such a flurry of excitement that they could hardly follow what he was saying. Telepathic communication was virtually impossible and dissolved into static cracklings in their heads.

Liberty wished that Zanny and their mother had been there, but as women they were forced to wait in a special room along with Aunt Honey and Molly and Charly. The official press conference would be held in this room following the announcement, although there were some members of the press in attendance at the dinner.

Now, after the preliminaries of calling the meeting to order, Mr. Boggles was getting to the heart of the matter. "A discovery of unparalleled importance to Holmesian scholarship has recently come to light." A wave of "ahhhs" rolled over the room. Mr. Boggles flushed with anticipation and importance. He was obviously relishing his moment as the announcer. "What would you say if I were to tell you that before "The Adventure of the Speckled Band," before even *The Sign of Four*, there was a draft of another work that combined the central themes of both these stories?"

"Oooohs" now began to hover in the air like a flock of starlings. The tension in the room mounted. People stopped eating their desserts and set down their forks. "Furthermore," Mr. Boggles continued, "what would you say if I were to tell you that Conan Doyle, the master of detective fiction, the creator of Professor Moriarty, the most perfect villain in literature, had, as a kind of sketching exercise, created another villain—one who failed miserably in literary terms?"

There was a gasp and then a hush. "We have heard rumors of him, haven't we?" He nodded knowingly at his audience. "A brief appearance in a badly damaged second draft discovered in a wet basement in the village of Stokes Poaches. The name in that draft was Morebutt—Nigel Morebutt."

Morebutt, flashed Liberty, and she and July nearly

giggled out loud. *We can't giggle, J. B. Remember what Shadrach said about villains hating to be laughed at?*

But Morebutt, Liberty? You know he did sort of have a fat . . .

Don't say it, J. B., we'll blow everything if we start laughing. She was biting the inside of her cheeks. She would bite them all night if she had to, but she would not laugh.

Boggles was continuing. "As this new find will doubtlessly prove, his characterization was so atrocious that he cannot be considered even as a forerunner to the infamous Moriarty—second-rate all the way." When Boggles said "second-rate," Liberty and July looked at one another. There had been a tiny crackling of static in their heads and then just the dim echo of a sigh. They both felt it.

He's gone, I think, Liberty flashed.

His secret's out.

Not exactly his secret, really. You can't blame the character for the bad writing.

And that seemed to be what Boggles was now saying. "This offers proof that Doyle indeed had his weaker moments as a writer. No one, however, can doubt his perseverance and ability to learn from past mistakes and disasters—the true mark of a pro. But perhaps beyond all this, and most fascinating of all—" Boggles paused, and his bushy salt-and-pepper eyebrows hiked clear up to his shiny bald head as he widened his eyes in anticipation of his next announcement—"is the revelation of . . ."

He's milking this for all he can, July flashed. Boggles inhaled deeply. The people were sitting on the edges of their seats. "Well, what would you say if I were to tell you that there was at one time another brother to Sherlock, indeed, a twin brother named Shadrach?"

A hush fell over the audience, and Liberty and July could hear the breath lock in some men's throats as they listened to these astonishing revelations. "And what would you say if I were to tell you that this other brother Shadrach was indeed a master of the science of detection, but preferred induction as his method over deduction?"

"Astounding!" Liberty heard someone murmur.

"Gentlemen, it gives me great pleasure to announce to you the discovery of a long-lost manuscript of Sir Arthur Conan Doyle, written early in his career when he was living on Devonshire Place. The elements I have just mentioned are all to be found in this manuscript. The manuscript has been authenticated and evaluated by Mr. Robeson Andrews from the firm of Andrews and Andrews and Mr. Philpot Kingsley, renowned Holmesian scholar, as you well know. Tonight I would like to present to you the young American discoverers of this manuscript who, in a supreme twist of what seems ironic fate, are themselves identical twin brothers—July and Liberty Starbuck." A deafening roar of applause and cheers filled the room.

At this point Liberty and July, accompanied by two security guards from Lloyd's of London, were to walk up to the podium with the manuscript and officially present it to the secretary of the society. But neither of them seemed to hear the thunderous ovation that was being accorded them. They seemed immune to the fact that they were about to be the most famous twins in London, heroes in the world of literature. Both of their minds were back at Number 3, Devonshire Mews as they walked the distance to the podium bearing their precious package.

Do you think he's going to make it?

That last rosette from his cravat just haunts me. I couldn't tell if it was his last glow, like an ember dying in a cold fire, or what.

I don't know. Do you think he could somehow feel his name being spoken from here, this distance? I mean, listen—everybody seems to be saying it now. Can't you hear it?

Indeed the name Shadrach was on everyone's lips and buzzed through the air. They could still hope.

Liberty and July were now at the podium. Together they spoke the piece they had been told to say, the words put in their mouths like dialogue written by an author for a character.

"Honorable Mr. Secretary, it gives us great pleasure to present to you, as a guardian for all people of the English-speaking world, these original words as written by Sir Arthur Conan Doyle, creator of Sherlock Holmes, the greatest detective in fiction."

They had done it. Mr. Boggles was now going to open the floor to limited questioning. There would be time for more questions at the press conference following the meeting. Liberty and July had carefully rehearsed their answers with Zanny. All references to literary ghosts actually able to materialize had been carefully deleted, but as many references to Shadrach as a prototype and the possessor of many of the skills now attributed to Sherlock were included. Also they hoped to be able to insert a few remarks about the twin detectives' differences in thinking styles and logic.

This was their chance to rescue Shadrach from the purgatorial existence of a literary stillborn. They were doing a very good job. They could tell that Mr. Boggles, the officers of the club, their own father, and Jonathan Swan were quite proud of them. July was getting more and more relaxed as the questioning proceeded, but he could tell Liberty was growing more and more tense. He couldn't figure out what was bothering her.

What's wrong?

You'll see soon enough.

What do you mean?

Don't get mad at me, promise, Liberty pleaded.

What do you mean—promise?

Just promise, and remember Shadrach said it was okay.

All right. But what's going to happen?

The plot is going to thicken! The game is afoot!

And with that, Liberty nimbly doffed her deerstalker cap and sent it flying across the room. Skimming under the crystal chandeliers, it landed at the table where Putnam was sitting. He smiled as it settled on a centerpiece. The audience gasped when they saw

Liberty's hair fall down to her shoulders. She then pulled off her chino pants and shirt and stood before the Blue Carbuncles in a smart plaid dress.

"I'm me," she said quietly. "Liberty Bell Starbuck, twin sister of July and co-discoverer of the Shadrach manuscript. I can't be anyone else. Just like Shadrach couldn't have been anybody else. I'm just plain me."

The audience gasped. And Putnam Starbuck, with tears running down his face, whispered: "*Sui Veritas Primo.*"

28

Born on the Fourth of July

THE CLAMOR WENT ON for days. Every newspaper printed headlines of the incredible discovery, with pictures of the manuscript and the twins. There were stories that focused not only on the discovery of the long-lost manuscript but on Liberty's daring feat in defying that bastion of English male chauvinism.

**LET FREEDOM RING
AND LIBERTY SINGS**

Old Fogies Shocked as Twelve-year-old Girl Breaks Barriers at One of London's Oldest Clubs

Another headline read:

**PETTICOATS INVADE
VENERABLE CARLTON CLUB**

A secretary had to be hired to handle the requests for television appearances and interviews with the twins. Liberty and July were on the cover of every major magazine—*Newsweek, Time, People, The London Illustrated News. Ms.* sent a photographer to take a picture of Liberty. She was to be a feature story entitled "Born on the Fourth of July: The Meaning of Independence!"

The twins were not only the focus of the media, but everyone wanted to meet them, including the queen of England. They were presented to the queen in her court at Buckingham Palace, and they were also invited to dinner by the heirs of Sir Arthur Conan Doyle.

The little twins were not neglected, either. The tabloids were enamored of them, and they appeared on the front page of several in their Davy Crockett coonskin caps and sometimes their press-on nails, under headlines like "Stranger than Fiction," or "Super Family Produces Two Sets of Amazing Twins."

Aunt Honey managed to get her mug into a fair number of magazine and newspaper pictures. There was even one photograph of her as an Ice Capades skater, and she had tried to get an interview about herself in *Ice World*, a magazine for skaters. But all the editor wanted to know was whether the twins, all four of them, skated and if there were any pictures of them on skates available.

Through it all, no one had breathed a word to anybody about the actual manifestation of Shadrach the literary ghost. This was their secret, for it was essential that Shadrach now live in the minds of readers as a literary character. Copies of the story had been reproduced in excerpts for journals and newspapers, and there were plans to publish the whole story in its rough-draft form with commentary. This was the way it should be—neat and proper.

When they had returned from the press conference that eventful evening, the entire family had been in high, soaring spirits. But as Liberty and July entered the house they had felt a sudden and sharp sadness. The shadows had receded from Number 3, Devonshire Mews, and Shadrach's presence was no longer felt. But they had a telepathic feeling that even if he had vanished, he had not died. Yet they looked for some sign that he was indeed resting in peace, no longer a literary stillborn. The sadness lingered with them for days.

And then one night he came back to them, all of his rosettes radiant, his waistcoat expanded with pride, the tassels on his smoking cap jiggling with delight. He had come back for a last visit and to make sure that they understood clearly about Simon.

29

Shadrach Returns: The Last Mission

IT WAS AN UNEXPECTED TIME of day for Shadrach to manifest himself, for it was early in the evening and still light outdoors. It was twilight really, the time before darkness falls but after the sun sets. The sky and air had been drained of the illuminating light of the day. It was now that smudgy hour near dinnertime when parents often tell children to be careful riding bicycles, for bike lights do not show up well, and in the dwindling light one's vision plays tricks.

It had begun to drizzle. A fine gray mist blew in from the western sea, the Atlantic. It carried warm, soft moisture from the gulfstream current, that special current of air that keeps England so green and makes roses bloom in December on the southwest coast.

Was it a trick of vision then that had been played on July and Liberty? They were alone in the garden room and had just fed the fish. Charly and Molly were out of the house, tagging along on a date with Zanny and Jonathan. Putnam was still at the embassy. The scent of jasmine filled the air, for the plants had grown as promised and now climbed the trellises on the north wall of the room. July and Liberty were standing by the garden room window, its panes barely wet and just beginning to be strung with the tiniest beads of water, when something streaked past outside the window.

It's him! July's thought teleblasted through the quiet of the garden room.

The boy?

Simon, July teleflashed and felt a lump in his throat.

And then the boy's face was at the window, pressing against the glass, streaked and dirty, yet no breath came to fog the pane. He had shining dark eyes, but they were not looking at the twins. He stared at the goldfish, whose bright orange shapes flashed through the pool under the lily pads with the tiny china villages that floated so serenely on the dark water. Then Simon lifted his eyes and looked directly at the twins. He had deep circles under his eyes, the kind of circles that worry parents when their children haven't gotten enough sleep.

He needs rest, both July and Liberty thought at once, just like a parent might say of a weary child.

Then another voice, a familiar voice, spoke.

> *I thought you'd never realize it, but I should have had more faith in you as authors.*

All the rosettes were glowing radiantly. One pump rested on the edge of the fish pool, and the tassels on his smoking cap were swinging.

Shadrach! they teleflashed together.

> *You didn't think I would just go off completely without saying thank you and good-bye and assuring you that I shall now rest in peace?*

But what about Simon? July asked.

Precisely, Shadrach replied.

He's a character without control, Liberty said.

> *Oh, and my dear, you don't know how many first drafts and second drafts the poor boy has been cut from. Not only Conan Doyle. You realize, don't you, that he began his career as a Bow Street Runner, or rather a street waif helping the Bow Street Runners. He appeared in a first draft of a book of fiction called* Richmond *that was published in 1827, during the heyday of the runners. He got cut from that. Doyle must have found a reference, or perhaps even found the first draft of that book. In any case he tried to revive him over fifty years later, albeit in a very small part. But nonetheless there was hope for Simon.*
>
> *But then Doyle cut him! Alas! This poor child has wended his way through many plots, seen more street action than crooks and bobbies four times his*

age, but he always gets cut, and none of these drafts has ever been found.

So it's up to us? July asked.

The rosettes of Shadrach's cravat shimmered radiantly. The twins could feel the energy in the air.

Indeed it is! Shadrach replied.

The three of them ascended to the attic room. July and Liberty went to the desk. From the drawer they took out a pad of paper, two pencils, and some jelly beans. Liberty placed several jelly beans on the tape dividing the desk. July sharpened the pencils. They did these simple tasks with great solemnity—a gravity that one might associate with priests or rabbis or any men and women who helped perform rituals of things sacred. But the twins were not praying. They were writing. They were not thinking of sacred words, but very ordinary words, and they were not describing rituals, but life, a life as portrayed in literature.

"This is the story of Simon." July began to write the words. "He was the last of the Baker Street Irregulars. There were always thought to be six of these children, but in fact there were seven." He stopped writing and looked up at Liberty and spoke. "Let's call this 'The Final Problem.' "

"Remember when Sherlock wrestles with Moriarty at Reichenbach Falls? It can be after that," Liberty suggested.

"You're right." July scratched his head. "Sherlock

was missing for three years after that. Everyone thought he was dead."

"Except Simon. Simon knew!"

"That's it!" July exclaimed and picked up the pen again. "Simon knew," he wrote.

"No," said Liberty, scowling. "We can't quite come right out and say it. We've got to begin to build more of a picture of his character." She took up the pen. "The first two sentences that you wrote are fine about this being the story of Simon, but we do need more of a picture of him. How Sherlock might have seen him after returning secretly from the falls."

She paused, bit the pencil. They felt a stir in the air around them. The rosettes seemed to be clustering near their heads and brushing their cheeks, and then, one by one, they simply flickered out.

He's gone, Liberty flashed.

Yes.

I think he's happy we remembered Simon.

Yes, but I miss him, don't you?

Yes. She paused in her thoughts. *I guess we just have to keep on writing. After all, Simon should be able to rest too.*

Liberty began to write, "No one knew Holmes was in London, and when the boy first appeared on the wet streets he looked like a smudge on a freshly rinsed world that summer morning. . . ."

The twins continued to write. And like the best of writers, they wrote from that deepest part of their hearts and brains, feeling the ache of missing one character, but learning to love a new one.

The Starbuck Family Album

Introducing the characters from* Double Trouble Squared*, the first book in the Starbuck Family Adventure Series. HBJ and Kathryn Lasky asked the Starbuck family to introduce themselves. . . .

■ JULY BURTON STARBUCK

AGE: 11
WEIGHT: *Are you sure you really want to know this? Oh well, why not. 79 pounds. I know, I'm kind of skinny.*
HEIGHT: 59¼ inches
PLACE OF BIRTH: Washington, D.C.

I cannot believe this publisher is making me write about myself. So where is the author, Kathryn Lasky, when we need her? If they only knew what it's like being a sixth grader. I have a major geography test next week. It's on the whole world. Well, not quite, but most of it. And now this on top of everything. I know, I can just hear my parents saying "Don't procrastinate, just do it." Okay, okay already, but I do just want to say one thing. Do you know how tough it is being a kid, having these adults boss you around all the time?

I was born exactly one minute after midnight on the Fourth of July. That's why my name is July. My nickname is J. B. or Jelly Bean. My twin sister, Liberty, was born exactly four minutes after me. And don't believe that stuff about girls maturing faster than boys. She's been trying to close the gap ever since.

You should also know that I love Sherlock Holmes and all the stories Conan Doyle wrote about him. I am not big on team sports. Aside from brussels sprouts, there's nothing I really hate. I do find many things annoying—like my littlest sisters, Molly and Charly, who are also twins.

I guess one of the most important things you should know about me and all the Starbuck children is that we have mental telepathy. We call it teleflashing. The link is strongest within each set of twins, but we can cross-communicate with the other twins as well. We know if the other person is really scared or in trouble or happy. We can say things to each other in a roomful of adults, and they never know what we're talking about. But most important, it's just kind of a nice feeling. Liberty and I never have to say hello or goodbye because we are always sort of connected, and because of this we never feel truly alone.

■ LIBERTY BELL STARBUCK

AGE: 11
WEIGHT: 79 pounds
HEIGHT: 59¼ inches
PLACE OF BIRTH: Washington, D.C.

Please note that I do not make a big deal about listing my weight, nor am I carrying on about this perfectly reasonable request from the publisher. I also think July is being a tad hard on Kathryn. We owe her a lot, and she shouldn't have to do everything. She knows what it's like to be a sixth grader—she has one. So much for the four-minute gap he insists shall never be closed. I think it is immediately apparent that I am taking a much more mature attitude toward this request than he is. We all have a lot of homework. He at least doesn't have to write a skit for social studies on the Pilgrims. Muriel Braverman—she's my best friend—and I do. I don't mean to sound unpatriotic, but every year since first grade we have spent the entire fall on the Pilgrims. There is a good chance we could enter high school and not know anything about the rest of the history of the world—like Napoleon and Waterloo or the Punic Wars and Hannibal and all that stuff. I also have a major math test coming up.

Because I was born at five minutes after midnight on the Fourth of July, my parents thought Liberty Bell was the perfect name for a baby girl. Okay, things I like and things I hate: I like Sherlock Holmes as much as my brother does. I am very interested in the biology of twins. I know a lot about it, and I know a lot about famous twins in history. There are places in the world where twins were worshiped as gods. There are other places where twins were thought to be bad luck, and they used to put them out on hillsides to die or be eaten by wolves. I am very thankful I was born in Washington, D.C., and that my parents think twins are neat. My mom is a twin. Her sister, Honey, is, to put it mildly, a difficult person and they are not at all alike. They never had the mental telepathy that we have. That's lucky. I wouldn't want to get too far into Aunt Honey's head.

I wish I were smarter in math, and could see things more clearly, the way July does with story problems, but he wishes he were better at English. And even though July can be very annoying, I'm glad I have the kind of brother I never have to say hello or good-bye to and that wherever we go in the world, we'll never feel really lonely.

■ **CHARLOTTE STARBUCK**

AGE: 5
WEIGHT: 46 pounds
HEIGHT: 44 inches
PLACE OF BIRTH: Charlotte Amalie, on the island of Saint Thomas, American Virgin Islands

Belly buttons. Pig guts. Galactic fish heads. Baa Baa, Black Sheep, have you any wool? Yes sir, yes sir, three belly buttons full. One for my master. One for my dame. And one for the little boy who lives down the drain with the itsy bitsy spider. Pig guts.

My mom said it was wrong to put my Christmas list in this thing we got to write. So I wrote it in code. The rest I'll write regular.

My name is Charlotte, but everyone calls me Charly. My sister Molly and I were named for a beautiful island in the Caribbean Sea. We were born there. We are identical twins. We are about the most identical twins Dr. Goldspoon has ever seen. We are called mirror-image identical twins, which means that when I look at Molly, it's like looking in a mirror. My cowlick goes one way, and Molly's goes the other. I have a birthmark on my left ear, and Molly has one on her right ear. See?

We both have very red hair, and we both love hair mousse. Grandma gave us Davy Crockett coonskin caps, and they are about the most favorite things we own. We wear them all the time, even in the summer if the temperature is under a hundred degrees.

Molly and I like to work on our Toilet Roll Kingdom. We've been building it since we were four. We make houses and people and buildings out of those cardboard things inside rolls of toilet paper. But the most important thing you should know about me is that I am one minute older than Molly.

■ **AMALIE STARBUCK**

AGE: 5
WEIGHT: 46 pounds
HEIGHT: 44 inches
PLACE OF BIRTH: Charlotte Amalie, on the island of Saint Thomas, American Virgin Islands

Charly might be one minute older, but look who had to put her Christmas list in this thing we have to write, even after Mom told her not to. That's being a baby, if you ask me. People call me Molly. That's short for Amalie. I got that name because it's the second word in the name of the town where we were born, and I came out one minute later than Charly. Ever since, Charly has never stopped trying to push ahead of me. It's no fair. And she is always messing with my *Bride Magazine* collection, and it's mine. At least most of it is, because I started collecting before Charly did. I got the mumps three days before Charly, and Grandma was visiting. She felt sorry for me and bought me a *Bride Magazine*.

People say we are *very* smart for our age. We are. And Mrs. Marlowe, our kindergarten teacher, told Mom that I am a bit more mature than Charly. So there, fat face, you and your big fat one minute!

■ **MADELINE STARBUCK**

Kathryn said that if you're over thirty-five, you do not have to give your age and weight. So that's me. Over thirty-five, mother of Molly and Charly, Liberty and July. You see I am very fair. I don't always make the younger ones come second. We take turns in our family, or at least we try to.

I am married to Putnam Starbuck. We're both from the Midwest, and we both went to the University of the Prairie. Unfortunately, it is often called P. U. I was a dance major. I come from a family of ballet teachers and dancers. My mom ran a little ballet school in Heart's Full, Kansas, where I grew up. My twin sister, Honey, was a dancer, too; she became a champion ice skater and later joined the Ice Capades.

When Putnam and I were first married and living in Washington, D.C., I taught ballet part-time. But after the first twins were born, I realized that going into business would be easier than getting back into my old leotard. I was always pretty good with a needle and thread, so I started Starbuck Recital Wear right in our house with an old Singer sewing machine and three-quarters of a mile of cerise and lime green ruffles. Well, word spread, and, as they say, the rest is history. Putnam claims you couldn't sit down anyplace around here without having a sequin stick to you. I had seamstresses and designers crawling all over the house, so we moved the whole business into a factory warehouse in Chevy Chase.

It's tough to do all this while trying to be a good mom, too, but Putnam is the greatest husband in the world and does half the cooking. Thank goodness for Zanny the Nanny. Now the kids can travel with their dad, and Zanny is there to watch over them. She's their teacher, too. They always take their schoolwork with them, but her speciality seems to be adventure.

■ PUTNAM STARBUCK

I understand I don't have to divulge my weight or age here. I'm plump, that's fairly obvious. And there is no hiding my baldness. I try not to hide anything. As you will learn in the Starbuck Adventures, our family motto is *Sui Veritas Primo*. That's Latin for Truth to Self First. It is not an old family motto. I made it up myself when I was in high school and started to go bald. It has served me and my family well in life. It is especially important in a family like ours, where there are two pairs of twins. Now that is probably the last time you will ever hear me refer to Liberty and July and Charlotte and Amalie as "sets" or "pairs." It rankles me to no end when people do this. These four children are not bookends. Nor are they shoes, socks, or mittens. They are individual human beings with very distinct personalities.

But enough about them. Now me. I have always worked for the government in one way or another. I was trained as a journalist and also went to law school. When Kathryn first discovered our family I had just quit my job with the Central Intelligence Agency. I wasn't a spy. My job was in the legal department, but then one day they asked me to wear a wig, don a mustache, and use a voice changer. I quit. Remember the family motto! How could I be true to myself with a wig, a mustache, and a voice changer? So I was out of work, and I loved it. My family, however, didn't love it. So I got a new job.

I think my kids are terrific. That's not to say they're perfect. I do think Molly and Charly could help a little more around the house. They're always talking about wanting chores like the kids in *Little House on the Prairie,* but they find our chores boring. They want a cow to milk! I also think July could worry about personal hygiene a little bit more, and Liberty could worry about it a little less. It seems as if Liberty washes her hair twice a day, July about once a month. But all in all they're good kids, and, yes, having four kids who are all twins is double trouble—but it's also double fun.

■ KATHRYN LASKY

July, I'll tell you where I've been: helping my twelve-year-old son write a report for school. And then, as if that's not bad enough, his best friend calls up and needs a topic sentence for a composition he has to do on—you guessed it, Liberty—the Pilgrims. And I had already helped my eight-year-old daughter do one of these Pilgrim things. I have been doing Pilgrim reports since . . . well, I can't tell you, because then you'll figure out my age. Let's just say it's running into the decades.

You want to know what else happened today? My daughter lost part of her science project. You want to know what part? This is kind of gross. The skull! It was the skull of a mouse that had been eaten by an owl. Owls can't digest the bones and the fur so they throw it up, and it comes out in this little furball, and if you take it apart carefully with tweezers, as my daughter did, you can find all these pieces of bone. She had a very nice little mouse skull. But it disappeared. We finally found it. Guess where? In my pocketbook, which was on the kitchen table. Actually it was in my checkbook. Is that weird? This is not the end of the story. The kids are now refusing to eat dinner. I made this sort of hamburger casserole thing, and they say they can't eat now. All they can think of is that owl throwing up the mouse stuff. I'll tell you, it's tough being a mom and trying to do all this dumb homework, and make dinner, and write books. Thank goodness I have a wonderful husband, Chris Knight. He makes documentary films and is a still photographer. He can cook, and he's as good as July is in math, so he can help the kids with their math homework. He's cute, too, and not bald yet.